SANDY STEELE ADVENTURES

Sandy Steele Adventures

SECRET MISSION TO ALASKA

BY ROGER BARLOW

SIMON AND SCHUSTER
New York, 1959

LIBRARY OF CONGRESS CATALOG CARD NUMBER: 59–13882
MANUFACTURED IN THE UNITED STATES OF AMERICA
BY H. WOLFF BOOK MFG. CO., INC., NEW YORK

CONTENTS

Secret Mission
to Alaska

CHAPTER ONE

Off to Alaska

SANDY STEELE twisted his lanky six-foot frame in the cramped airplane seat, stretching his long legs out in the aisle. Yawning, he glanced out of the small, round window beside him. Although it was daylight now, the ground was completely hidden by a layer of dense clouds that stretched away to the horizon on all sides like fluffy marshmallow topping. The sound of the motors was a dull, monotonous throbbing in his ears.

Sandy leaned forward and ruffled the black crew cut that was just visible over the top of the seat ahead of him. "Hey, Jerry, you awake?"

"Yeah," a voice mumbled sleepily, "I'm awake. Are we going to land yet?"

"I don't know." Sandy looked across the aisle at his father, who was just lighting his pipe. "How about it, Dad?"

Dr. John Steele studied his watch thoughtfully. "Oh, I'd say about another half hour."

The steward, an army corporal, walked back from the forward compartment with a tray of paper cups. "Coffee, anyone?"

The steaming-hot black liquid cleared the cobwebs out of Sandy's head, and he began to look forward with excited anticipation to their arrival in Canada.

"Will Professor Crowell meet us at the airport?" he asked his father.

Dr. Steele nodded. "Yes. Then we'll drive back to his place and pick up his dog team."

Jerry James's granite-jawed face appeared over the back of the seat as he knelt, facing Sandy. "What's this about dogs?"

"Berkley Crowell breeds sled dogs as a hobby," Dr. Steele explained. "Eskimo huskies. He's taking his prize team up to Alaska to compete in the annual race from Whitehorse to Skagway."

"Hey, that sounds like fun," Jerry said.

"As a matter of fact," the doctor went on, "that will be one of your major jobs on this expedition. You boys will drive the truck with the dogs and help the professor with their care and feeding."

Dr. Steele turned his attention back to his book as Sandy and Jerry got into a conversation with the young corporal who had served the coffee.

"Both you fellows from California?" the corporal asked. "Whereabouts?"

"Valley View," Sandy told him. "That's near San Diego, but more inland."

"I have a cousin in the Navy," the corporal said. "He was stationed at San Diego. Nice country." He grinned. "You guys are going to find the climate of Alaska a lot different than California."

Jerry shivered. "You're telling us!"

"You go to school in Valley View?" the corporal asked.

"High school," Sandy told him. "We're both juniors."

"How long are you going to be in Alaska?"

"About three weeks, I guess. It's the Christmas vacation, and my dad got our principal to let us take an extra week on account of the educational value of this expedition we're going on."

The corporal looked interested. "What kind of an expedition is it?"

"My dad is a United States government geologist," Sandy explained. "This expedition is part of a long-range Canadian-American project to chart glacial movements during the Ice Age. We'll be collecting soil, rock and ore samples on our way through western Canada and Alaska."

"Sounds like fun," the corporal said. "You'll get a kick out of Alaska. It's a great place. I've flown up there a couple of times."

"What's our forty-ninth state like, anyway?" Jerry asked curiously. "We bought it from the Indians for twenty-four dollars, didn't we?"

Sandy and the corporal laughed. "That was Manhattan Island, you dope!" Sandy said. "We bought Alaska from the Russians for about $7,000,000."

"It's twice as big as Texas," the corporal told them, "but the population is only a little over 200,000. And most of these people have only been there since the end of World War Two."

"I guess we never would have realized just how valuable Alaska is if the Japanese hadn't tried to attack us across the Aleutian Islands," Sandy said.

At that moment, a buzzer sounded and the green light at the front of the cabin began to flash. "Oh-oh," the corporal said. "Looks like we're getting ready to land. Fasten your seat belts, folks." He turned and hurried forward.

Dr. Steele stood up and removed his mackinaw from the overhead rack. As he did so, a big, black, ominous-looking .45 Colt automatic slipped out of one of the pockets and crashed to the floor.

The boys' eyes widened and Sandy blurted out in shocked surprise, "Where did you get that, Dad?"

Dr. Steele retrieved the gun hastily and stuck it back into his pocket. "Oh—er—something a friend advised me to bring with me. In case we get a chance to do any hunting," he added.

Sandy frowned. "Hunting with an *automatic!* That's crazy, Dad. Wouldn't a rifle have been more practical?"

A thin smile spread the doctor's lips. "I suppose you're right. I should have consulted you before I got it."

"Just where *did* you get it, Dad?" Sandy asked suspiciously. "The Colt .45 automatic is an official U.S. Army sidearm."

There was just the faintest trace of irritation in Dr. Steele's voice when he answered. "All these questions! You're beginning to sound like your Aunt Vivian. . . . Look, we had better fasten our safety belts. We're going to land."

"Sure, Dad, sure," Sandy said. There was something uncommonly mysterious about his father's behavior, and it worried him.

CHAPTER TWO

A Hint of Trouble

The big U.S. Army transport touched down at the R.C.A.F. military airstrip at Fort St. John, British Columbia, shortly after dawn on December 23. Dr. Steele and his party were groggy after spending a restless night of fitful slumber on the hard, uncomfortable canvas seats that were slung along the walls of the plane's huge, drafty cabin. But the first bite of the dry-ice bitter air of the Canadian winter snapped them wide-awake and alert.

"Wow!" Jerry exclaimed, bundled up like a bear in his hooded parka. "It must be at least one thousand degrees below zero."

Dr. Steele smiled. "You think this is cold? Just wait until we get farther up north."

Lou Mayer, Dr. Steele's assistant, groaned. "When does the next plane leave for California?" He broke into a fit of uncontrollable shudders. A dark, mild-mannered young man in his late twenties, Lou had been born in Texas and spent half of his life in Southern California. He consequently had little tolerance for the cold.

Sandy grinned superciliously. "You guys should have been smart like me. I wore my long red flannels."

"That's a good point," Dr. Steele said. "In this country, proper clothing is essential to survival. It's as vital as sufficient food and drink. You must start conditioning yourselves to think about it."

Abruptly, they all became aware that Jerry was staring with hypnotic fixity toward the edge of the landing field.

"Hey!" Sandy asked. "What gives with you? What are you looking at?"

Jerry's eyes were glazed. Dumbly he raised one arm and pointed at the mountains of snow banked at the sides of the field. Finally he managed to mumble, "Snow. That's snow?"

"Of course it is. You act as if you never saw it before."

Jerry nodded, wide-eyed. "I never did."

Sandy and the two men broke out laughing. "Well, this is an occasion," Dr. Steele said. "I promise you you will have your fill of it before we're through with this trip."

Jerry was flabbergasted. "I've seen pictures of it, but I just never realized there could be so much of it in one place. Man! That one drift must be twenty feet high. Can you imagine waking up some morning in Valley View and finding that in your front yard, Sandy?"

"Well, I haven't seen too much of it," Sandy admitted. "But I've been up to the Northwest with Dad a few times."

At that moment a jeep screeched to a stop nearby, its exhaust spewing out smoke like a chimney. The corporal at the wheel leaned out and yelled to them. "Dr. Steele here?" After the geologist identified himself, the corporal told them to pile into the jeep. "There's a gent waiting for you at headquarters. A detail will be right out to unload your baggage."

"How do you keep these runways free of ice?" Dr. Steele shouted to the driver above the loud, rowdy roar of the little jeep motor.

"Sweep 'em with giant vacuum cleaners regularly," the corporal replied. "When it gets really rough we melt the ice with flame throwers."

Professor Berkley Crowell was waiting for them close by the glowing steel-drum coal stove that reinforced the electric heaters in the big quonset-hut headquarters. "You can't beat the old-fashioned way," he said with a smile, toasting his fingers in the shimmering heat waves that radiated from the top of the steel drum.

The professor was a slight, stooped, very British-looking man in his middle fifties. He had a thin weatherbeaten face, a sharp nose and a close-cropped mustache. His deep-set blue eyes were warm and full of good humor.

"Well," he said, upon being introduced to Sandy and Jerry, "I understand that you boys will be helping me with my dog team."

"We'll do the best we can, sir," Sandy told him.

"They won't give you too much trouble," the professor said. "Titan—that's my lead dog—he practically runs the whole show himself. Possesses human intelligence, that animal."

"When do we get to see them?" Jerry asked.

"As soon as we get back to my ranch. I'm situated about ten miles down the Alaska Highway,

toward Dawson Creek. That's the southern termi-
nus of the highway."

When they had finished the steaming mugs of
hot coffee served up by the flying officers' mess,
Professor Crowell and his party climbed aboard
the big station wagon parked in the drive and
drove away from the air base.

The Alaska Highway was a broad, smooth,
gravel-topped road hewed through some of the
thickest forests and most rugged terrain on the
North American continent. Now the gravel was
topped by a thick crust of snow.

"A miracle of our century," Professor Crowell
explained as they drove. "Built in just eight
months by your amazing U.S. Army engineers in
1943, when the Japanese forces were threatening
the Aleutian Island chain. It was a lifesaving
artery to Alaska and a vital chain to our western
air bases. Sixteen hundred and seventy-one miles.
Just imagine!"

An auto filled with shouting children whizzed
past them, traveling in the opposite direction. It
was weighted down with valises and bundles
strapped to the roof and fenders.

"Where are they going?" Jerry inquired.

"Pioneer settlers for your glorious forty-ninth
state," Professor Crowell answered. "There's a

steady stream of them. Did you know that the population of Alaska has tripled since World War Two?"

"It sort of gives you goose pimples," Sandy said. "It's almost as if you turned back the clock a hundred years."

"The last frontier of the United States," Dr. Steele remarked. "On this planet, at least."

"When will we be leaving, Professor Crowell?" Lou Mayer asked.

The professor glanced down at his wrist watch. "It's eight o'clock now. I estimate we'll be on our way shortly after noon. I want you fellows to get a hot meal into you first. Then we'll load the truck and station wagon." He looked around at Dr. Steele. "We'll pick up your equipment at Fort St. John on the way back."

Jerry was fascinated by the high banks of snow on the shoulders of the road. "Boy, I wonder how they keep this thing open. Back in the States we're always reading about whole towns being cut off by a measly two feet of snow."

"Even big cities like New York," Sandy chimed in.

The professor smiled. "That's because cities like New York aren't prepared for heavy snowfalls. Up here, we expect it. Why, I bet a little village like

Dawson Creek has more snow equipment than most big cities on the eastern seaboard of the United States. Along the Alaska Highway, for instance, there are one hundred and twenty-five weather stations alone, and almost as many maintenance stations. No, you stand a better chance of getting marooned on the Pennsylvania Turnpike than you do on this road."

Professor Crowell's ranch house was located on a cutoff about a quarter of a mile from the main highway. It was a sprawling frame building with a large barn at the back of the property and completely surrounded by a thick spruce forest.

The professor, a widower, had twin daughters, Judy and Jill, who kept house for him. Their domestic efficiency made them seem older than their seventeen years. The girls were blond and blue-eyed and very pretty, and Jerry couldn't look at them without stammering and blushing. It was obvious he was smitten with the twins.

The Crowell household also included a middle-aged French couple, the Duprés; Henri took care of the livestock and his wife, Marie, did the cooking. Then there was Tagish Charley, who took care of the kennels.

Tagish Charley was a full-blooded Indian. He stood 6′ 4″ tall, weighed 230 pounds and was as lithe as a panther. His hair was the flat black color of charcoal, and his skin was the texture of ancient parchment. Charley could have been any age, from 40 to 400. He spoke English well enough, when he spoke, which was very seldom; and he said what he had to say in as few words as possible.

"Charley is economical with his money and his speech," Professor Crowell said when he introduced him to his guests. "He's as stoic as a cigar-store Indian."

Sandy and Jerry hit it off with Charley from the start. While the geologists went over the last-minute details of their trip in the professor's study, Charley took the boys out to the kennel at one side of the barn. A dozen husky dogs were frolicking in the snow inside a wire enclosure. As soon as they saw Charley they all rushed over to the gate and piled up in a seething mass of yelping, snarling, twisting fur, leaping up against the chain link fence and falling back on top of each other. It was a wild melee.

"Wow!" Jerry exclaimed. "They look as if they'd eat you alive."

The Indian grunted. "No hurt. They want to play."

Jerry looked dubious. "I bet they play rough."

The Eskimo dogs were handsome animals. In reality they weren't particularly large; probably they weighed about 75 to 80 pounds and stood 18 inches high at the shoulder; but with their broad chests, thick necks and massive heads they looked enormous. Their great thick coats varied in color from black-and-white to slate-gray, solidly and in combinations of all three. They had powerful wolflike muzzles, sharp ears and slanting eyes.

Tagish Charley opened the gate and motioned the boys to follow him into the pen. The dogs barked and leaped around the Indian, nipping his trousers and mittens playfully. They ignored the boys. There was one exception. Standing off to one side was a big, solid-black husky with a white mask across his eyes and upper muzzle. By far the largest dog of the lot—Sandy estimated his weight to be at least 100 pounds—he seemed to regard the antics of his fellows with regal aloofness. Finally his eyes turned solemnly on the boys and he started toward them.

"Charley!" Jerry yelled, grabbing Sandy's arm nervously. "He's charging us."

Sandy laughed. "Go on, you sissy. His tail is wagging. That means he wants to be friends."

"You know that, and I know that," said Jerry, edging backward, "but does *he* know that?"

"That Black Titan," Charley said. "Lead dog. Best husky in all the North."

As the big dog nuzzled against his leg, Sandy leaned down and stroked his broad, glossy head. "Nice feller. Good boy . . . Hey, where did you get that lump on your skull, Titan?"

"He save professor's life," Charley declared without emotion. "Bad man hit him on head with club."

"Bad man! When?" the boys exclaimed in a chorus.

"Five, six nights back. Titan hear prowler. Jump over fence. Man open window, climb into professor's room, choke professor. Titan jump through window, save him."

"What happened to the burglar? Did they catch him?" Sandy asked excitedly.

"No. He club Titan, dive through window into snow. Get away with dog team."

"Gee," Jerry said. "Even up here they got characters like that. Only instead of a getaway car, they use dog sleds."

"Did he get away with anything valuable?" Sandy asked.

The Indian's brown face seemed to grow even darker. "He no come to rob money."

"What do you mean?" Sandy asked.

Charley shrugged. "Many strange things happen here this year. Professor sleep with gun under his pillow."

Sandy and Jerry exchanged wondering looks. "Now who'd be out to get a nice old geezer like the professor?" Jerry wanted to know.

Sandy was thoughtful. "I don't know, Jerry. I don't know. But I have a feeling we're going to find a lot more excitement on this trip than we bargained for."

"I agree with you," a terse female voice said from behind them.

Surprised, Sandy whirled around to find Judy Crowell standing in the open gateway. Bundled up in ski pants, mackinaw and high boots, she might have been a boy, except for the mass of golden hair sticking out in tufts from beneath her wool cap.

"Charley's right," she said. "A lot of strange things have been happening around here during the last few months. Ever since Dad spent a week in Ottawa this fall, he's been a different man. He's lost weight. He can't sleep or eat. And—" she shivered—"he always carries a pistol with him. He's afraid of something—or someone. But when Jill and I ask him, he just laughs and says we've been seeing too many American motion pictures."

Sandy felt cold prickles creep up his back. "It's funny. My dad brought along a gun with him too."

Jerry whistled. "What's it all mean, Sandy?"

"I don't know, pal. But I don't like it."

Still surrounded by his ring of canine admirers, Tagish Charley addressed Judy Crowell. "You no worry about your papa, Miss Judy. Charley take good care of him. Bad fellers come around, me break 'em up like firewood." He made a twisting motion in the air with his two huge fists.

For some reason Sandy felt relieved. "I didn't know you were coming with us, Charley."

Charley's serious, expressionless face altered for a fleeting instant in a suggestion of a smile. "I just decide now."

CHAPTER THREE

A Mysterious Intruder

THE LITTLE CARAVAN headed north on the Alaska
Highway about 12:20 P.M. Professor Crowell, Dr.
Steele and Lou Mayer led the way in the big station wagon, which was loaded down with scientific
equipment and supplies. Sandy, Jerry and Tagish
Charley followed in a surplus U.S. Army six-by-six
truck. The boys and the Indian all rode in the
roomy cab, with Sandy at the wheel. The back of
the truck, roofed with a heavy canvas top, had
been converted into a comfortable compartment
for the professor's seven prize huskies. Here, also,
were the big dog sled, a pyramidal tent, sleeping
bags, cooking utensils and a Coleman stove.

As Professor Crowell pointed out, there were

tourist camps and aid stations all along the highway, but sometimes it was more convenient to set up one's own camp at the side of the road. Particularly in winter, travelers had to be prepared for emergencies.

Both vehicles were equipped with heavy-duty tire chains on all wheels, plus oversized snow tires, and they rode smoothly and firmly across the hard-packed snow surface of the highway.

As the afternoon deepened into an early dusk, the temperature plummeted, and the chill penetrated the cab of the truck, even though the heater was going full blast. Sandy doubled up his hands into fists inside his mittens and wriggled his feet inside his fur-lined boots to stimulate his circulation.

"I'm warm as toast except for my fingers and toes," he said.

Jerry fingered his nose gingerly. "My old schnozzola is getting numb."

Tagish Charley, who was taking his turn at the wheel, patted his stomach. "Belly say soon time to stop and eat."

Jerry yawned and looked at the dashboard clock. "Three-thirty," he announced. "We've been on the road for about three hours. How far have we come?"

Sandy studied the speedometer. "A little over one hundred and ten miles."

"That's pretty good," Jerry said. "We're averaging almost forty per."

A little while later they passed a river, and now Charley turned the headlights on. Out of nowhere, it seemed, thousands of tiny snowflakes swirled suddenly into the yellow cones of light.

"It's snowing!" Jerry exclaimed.

Sandy surveyed the wilderness on both sides anxiously. "I'd hate to spend the night out here in a blizzard."

"We stop soon," Charley assured him.

The words were scarcely out of his mouth when they rounded a curve and came upon a little settlement set back in a clearing in a pine grove. It consisted of two large quonset huts and three small log cabins. The warm glow of lights in the small windows of the buildings gave Sandy a feeling of well-being. The station wagon slowed down, tooted twice with its horn and swerved off the highway into the circular drive that had been plowed up to the entrance of the main building. As the truck's headlights swept across the front of the other larger quonset hut, they could see that it had big sliding doors that allowed one entire wall to open up like an airplane hangar. And as the lights probed the interior of the hut, they could make out a neat two-engine plane mounted on skis. The brief glimpse also revealed a big bulldozer plow and other snow-fighting machinery.

"Road crew," Charley told the boys. "They good fellers. We eat good, drink good and sleep good."

"You were so right, Charley," Jerry said later, as he pushed himself away from the big plank table after sharing a hearty meal of roast lamb, fried potatoes, home-made rolls and apple pie with Superintendent MacKensie and his maintenance gang. "I never ate so good." He polished off a pint mug of milk that was half cream and sighed. "Or drank so good either."

Superintendent MacKensie, a big florid-faced man, tugged at one side of his blond handlebar mustache. "Here now, you're not finished, are you?" he asked.

Jerry patted the round swell of his stomach. "If I ate another mouthful, I'd burst, sir."

"That's a shame," MacKensie said solemnly. "Now Cooky's feelings will be hurt and he'll make you wash the dishes."

A swarthy giant of a man at the far end of the

table pounded the planks with hamlike fists. "By gar, I weel!" he roared in mock anger. "You no like Frenchy's cooking?"

Everyone laughed as Jerry looked around uncertainly.

Dr. Steele patted his mouth with a napkin. "As Jerry so aptly put it, Frenchy, 'We never ate so good.'"

"We're happy you enjoyed it, Doctor," Superintendent MacKensie said. "Now if you'd like to go into the other room and toast your feet by the hearth, I'll have one of the lads stir up that fire in your cabin."

"An excellent suggestion," Professor Crowell agreed.

With the exception of a half dozen men of the road crew who had some tasks to attend to, they all retired to the large, comfortably furnished recreation room where an enormous stone fireplace almost covered one wall. Sandy, Jerry and Lou Mayer sat cross-legged directly in front of the blazing logs, on a thick bearskin robe that was spread-eagled on the floor.

"Man!" Jerry whispered in an awed voice, lifting the huge head and inspecting the gleaming fangs that were still frightening even in death.

"I think if I ever ran into one of these babies I'd just roll over and die before he laid a paw on me."

Lou Mayer poked one of the clawed forepaws with his toe. "Well, it's a sure bet you'd die if he ever *did* lay one of those paws on you. They're as big as dinner plates."

Superintendent MacKensie, slouched in an old-fashioned rocker, sucked his pipe gravely. "I've seen them kill a horse with one swipe."

"You've *seen* them?" Sandy asked.

MacKensie smiled reminiscently. "As a matter of fact *that* fellow did kill my horse. I was hunting with a party up on Kodiak Island. I blundered around a rock right into the beggar. He rose up on his hind legs, caught my horse with one blow in the choppers and that was it. I managed to jump free. Then I pumped five shots into him. They might as well have been darts. He would have got me for sure if the guide hadn't dropped him with a brain shot."

"Powerful beasts," Professor Crowell acknowledged. "The Roman Emperor Nero used to pit bears against lions in the arena. And frequently they killed the lions."

"It's a lucky thing we did bring all those guns along—" Jerry began, than caught himself as

Sandy and Lou Mayer stiffened visibly. "Well, it's a good idea with mankillers like this running loose," he finished lamely.

Superintendent MacKensie laughed. "So you expect to do some hunting while you're up north, do you?" he said to Professor Crowell. He turned to Dr. Steele. "Of course, the customs officials plugged up the barrels of your weapons, didn't they?"

"Yes, they did," Dr. Steele said emphatically. Speaking directly to Sandy and Jerry, he explained. "You see, the Canadians don't want visitors to shoot up their game preserves, and quite rightly so. When we cross the border into Alaska, the officials will remove the seals from the barrels. Do you *understand?*"

"Yes, sir," Sandy mumbled, looking quickly away into the embers. He was stunned. *Those automatics weren't plugged up.* He had never heard his father deliberately tell a lie before.

Unaware of the tension that had mushroomed up, MacKensie stretched. "I'd better be getting back to the radio shack and see what's come in from the weather stations on this storm. If she looks bad, I'll have to keep a crew on alert. Any time you gentlemen feel like sacking in, go to it. Your cabin should be warm now. It's small, but cozy. There are six bunk beds, so it won't be too crowded."

"Where's Charley?" Sandy asked, suddenly aware that the Indian was not in the room.

"Right after supper he went outside to get your dogs bedded down," one of the crewmen told him.

Professor Crowell smiled. "He treats them like children, and they love it. Actually, though, all those huskies need for a bed is a soft snowdrift."

"They like to sleep in snow?" Jerry asked incredulously. "Don't they freeze?"

"No, once they tuck in their paws and stick their noses under their tails, they're ready for anything. Have you noticed their coats? Double thick. Underneath that heavy outside fur there's a short woolly undercoat. The fact is they're probably more comfortable sleeping outside than next to a roaring fire."

Lou Mayer held his hands up to the flames. "We have nothing in common."

After MacKensie left, the other maintenance men began to drift off to bed. The snow was coming down very hard, and they faced the prospect of a long, hard day battling the drifts.

About nine o'clock, Sandy yawned and stretched. "What do you say we turn in, pal?" he said to Jerry.

"I'm with you," Jerry replied promptly.

The boys looked inquiringly at the older men. "You two run along," Dr. Steele told them. "We'll finish our pipes first."

Sandy and Jerry dug their mackinaws and mittens out of a heap of clothing on the long table in the vestibule and slipped on their boots.

"It's only a hundred-yard walk," Sandy admitted, "but at thirty below zero it's worth the trouble."

"Amen," Jerry agreed, wrapping his wool muffler around his lantern jaw.

The boys stepped out the back door of the big hut and followed the path leading back to the cabins. Ten feet away from the building, the wind-whipped grains of ice and snow closed in on them like a white curtain, blotting out their vision. If it had not been for the clearly defined path, they would have been helpless.

"You could get lost in your own back yard in this stuff," Jerry gasped. "Yipes!" he shouted as he blundered off the path into a snowdrift. "Where's the St. Bernards?"

Sandy took his arm and guided him back on the path. Finally, a dark outline with a faint square of light in the center of it loomed up before them.

"Here we are," Sandy shouted above the wind. "Home at last."

"If only the boys back at Valley View High could see us now," Jerry yelled in his ear. "Wouldn't it be something to drop that Pepper March out here some night? Boy! Or better yet, let's drop him into a den of those Kodiak bears."

Sandy laughed. "I don't know which of the two is more ornery. He might scare them off."

They reached the cabin door, and Sandy leaned against it and pushed it open. They staggered inside and slammed it shut behind them. The interior of the one-room shack was dark, except for the logs burning low and evenly on the open hearth.

Sandy blinked to accustom his eyes to the dimness. "I could have sworn there was a light in the window as we came along the path."

"Probably the reflection of the flames on the panes," Jerry suggested.

"Yeah. Well, let's light a lamp." Sandy took several steps toward a table silhouetted against the firelight, then stopped suddenly. "Hey!" he said in a startled voice, nudging an object on the floor with his boot. "What's this junk spread all over the floor? Looks like somebody was breaking up house.

I wonder—" He broke off as a dark shape material-
ized from the shadows in the far corner of the
cabin and seemed to glide toward him. At the same
time, he heard Jerry's excited shout in his ear.

"Sandy! There's somebody in here. Hey, look
out!"

Sandy Steele, without even a consciousness of
what he was facing, reacted with his athlete's in-
stinct and reflexes. Crouching low, he braced himself solidly, and as the figure loomed up before
him, he threw a hard body block at the middle of
it. His shoulder hit a solid form and he heard a
soft grunt of pain and anger. As his arms grap-
pled with the intruder, he realized for the first
time that it was a man. His fingers brushed rough
wool, and then he felt the steel fingers at his
throat.

"Get help, Jerry!" he bellowed, just before the
wind was pinched off in his throat. Then he took
a hard, numbing blow at the back of his neck and
felt himself falling . . . falling . . . falling . . .
into blackness.

CHAPTER FOUR

Charley Works Out the Huskies

WHEN SANDY REGAINED CONSCIOUSNESS he was lying flat on his back on a cot, surrounded by a ring of anxious faces. He recognized his father, Jerry, Professor Crowell, Lou Mayer, Superintendent MacKensie and several other men from the maintenance gang.

"What—what happened?" Sandy asked weakly.

"It's all right, Son. You're fine. Just a nasty bump on the head," Dr. Steele told him.

"He really clobbered you, Sandy," Jerry said. "Then he straight-armed me and sent me flying back over a chair. Before I could get up he was gone in the blizzard."

"There's no sense trying to follow him in this

heavy snow," MacKensie declared. "His tracks are probably covered already."

"Did he get away with anything?" Sandy wanted to know?

Dr. Steele and Professor Crowell exchanged significant glances. Then the Canadian geologist said hurriedly, "No, he didn't steal a thing. Probably some renegade trapper looking for guns and ammunition. They prey on unwary travelers, these chaps. I'll bet he's wanted by the Mounties as it is."

Superintendent MacKensie looked puzzled. "He certainly was a queer one, all right. He really messed things up. But, now, what do you suppose he was after in that stuff?" He pointed to an open valise in the middle of the room.

Sandy propped himself up on one elbow and saw that Professor Crowell's notebooks and papers were scattered all about the floor.

"He must have thought you had money hidden between the pages," Lou Mayer said quickly.

Superintendent MacKensie scratched his head. "I dunno. It beats me. We've never had anything like this happen before. There have been hijackings on the highway, but no one's ever had the nerve to break in here."

"Well, no harm done," Dr. Steele said. "And

Sandy will be as good as new after a night's sleep. I suggest we clean this mess up and turn in."

The others agreed, and while Sandy rested on the cot they began to gather up their scattered belongings.

"I wonder if he got at the rest of the stuff we left in the station wagon," Professor Crowell said.

"I doubt it," Superintendent MacKensie said. "Your wagon is in the shed with our scout plane and the heavy machinery. We've had men working out there all evening."

After the cabin was in order, MacKensie and his men said good night and went back to the main barracks. As they were undressing before the fire, Dr. Steele questioned Sandy casually but with painstaking thoroughness about his encounter with the intruder.

"Was he a big man?" the doctor asked. "Did you get a look at his face?"

Sandy shook his head. "It was too dark to see much of anything. All I know is that he was big, taller than me, and husky."

"That goes for me, too," Jerry agreed. "For all I know it could have been Tagish Charley."

Professor Crowell dropped the boot he was holding with a loud clatter. "What did you say, boy?" he asked in a tense voice.

Jerry laughed nervously at the professor's obvious dismay. "I mean he was big like Charley. Of course it wasn't Charley. Heck, it could have been that big French cook. All I know is that he was big and strong."

"By the way," Dr. Steele said suddenly, "where *is* Charley?"

No one answered for a long moment. Then Sandy said, "I guess he's still out with the dogs. Or maybe he's back swapping stories with the old-timers in the barracks."

Just as Lou Mayer was about to turn down the lamp, after the others were all in bed, the cabin door swung in and Tagish Charley tramped into the room. His hood and parka were encrusted with snow and ice, as were his boots and trousers. He looked as if he had been out in the storm for a long time. In the crook of his left arm he held a rifle.

"Good lord, Charley!" the professor exclaimed, sitting upright on his cot. "Where have you been, man?"

The Indian walked over to the fireplace and shook himself like a great dog. Carefully he leaned the rifle against the wall and shrugged out of his parka. "I drink coffee in kitchen with

Frenchy when man run in and say someone break into this cabin. I take rifle and follow him."

"In this storm!" Sandy said. "You could have gotten lost and frozen to death."

Charley grunted and tapped a finger to his temple. "Indian have thing up here like pigeon. Always find way home. Bad man have sled and dogs waiting in trees. No use follow him. If snow stop in morning, maybe I look around some more." He kicked off his boots, stepped out of his wet trousers and spread them out over the back of a chair near the fire. Then, like a big animal, he padded across the floor to an empty bunk. Seconds after his head hit the pillow, the rafters shook from his mooselike snores.

Jerry leaned over the side of his top-deck wall bunk and grinned at Sandy in the bunk underneath. "Now I know those guys up in Tibet are all wet. There isn't any Abominable Snowman. They bumped into Tagish Charley when he was out for one of his evening strolls."

Sandy grinned back, but it was a weak grin. He was bothered alternately by twinges of suspicion and pangs of guilt. It *couldn't* be Charley; he *knew* it! Yet, anything was possible.

The snow stopped during the night and a high-pressure area moved into the vicinity. Morning brought clear blue skies and bright sun. But the air was still dry and frosty.

"Actually, only about seven inches fell," Superintendent MacKensie told them at breakfast. "By the time you folks are on your way, the highway will be slick as a whistle. Our patrol plane's scouting back in the direction of Dawson Creek to see if any motorcars are in trouble. If anyone was on the road when that snow started coming down real hard, they would have had to sit it out overnight."

"I hope we're still here when the plane gets back," Jerry said. "I'd like to see how they land those babies on skis."

"Actually, it's smoother than landing on wheels," Professor Crowell told him. "I know I prefer them."

"Do you have your own plane, Professor?" Sandy asked.

"Oh, yes. In wild, big country like this, planes are more common than family cars, and far more practical. In the summertime almost every lake you pass on your way north looks something like a supermarket parking field. Private planes, all sizes and shapes and makes."

Jerry whistled. "Boy, that's the life. Can you

imagine how that would be back in Valley View?
I can just hear myself saying to my father, 'Hey,
Pop, I got a heavy date tonight. Can I have the
keys to the plane?' "

The men laughed and Professor Crowell said,
"That's not as much of a joke as you think. My
daughters are always flying up to Edmonton to
shop for their new spring outfits and Easter
bonnets."

Jerry looked wistful. "Gee, it must be more fun
being a kid up here than it is in the city."

Dr. Steele smiled. "It certainly must be more
exciting in some ways. Then again, I suspect that
youngsters like you and Sandy would miss your
malt shops, drive-ins and television."

"They have television here," Sandy said.

"Yes," Superintendent MacKensie admitted,
"but it's pretty limited compared to what you
Americans can see."

The boys were intrigued by the heavy, thick
flapjacks that Frenchy the cook served with thick
slabs of bacon.

"They taste different than what my maw
makes," Jerry commented. "Sort of sour." Then,
with an apologetic glance at the big, bushy-headed
cook, "But I love 'em."

Superintendent MacKensie's eyes twinkled.

"You may not believe it," he said, "but the fermented yeast dough that went into these flapjacks is over sixty years old."

Jerry choked in the middle of a bite and swallowed hard. "Sixty years old! You're kidding, sir?"

"Not in the least. It was handed down to Frenchy by his father, who was a gold prospector up in the Yukon in the eighteen-nineties."

"Wow!" Jerry laid down his fork. "Talk about hoarders."

Dr. Steele laughed. "Sourdough, of course. Those old prospectors got their nickname from it. You boys have heard of sourdoughs, haven't you?"

"Sure," Jerry admitted. "I just never knew where the name came from."

"Sourdough was the prospector's staff of life on the trail," Superintendent MacKensie explained. "Once he got the mixture just right, he'd keep it in a tightly closed container and add to it as he used it. But the culture always remained the same."

"Yeast is like a fungus," Professor Crowell elaborated for the boys' benefit. "It's composed of living, growing cells."

"Yes," the superintendent went on. "This particular strain in the flapjacks we're eating has been kept alive for sixty years by Frenchy's family."

"*Oui,*" the cook spoke from the end of the table. "My *papa* give some of this sourdough to all his sons and daughters when they leave home. I give to my son some day."

"Amazing," said Lou Mayer.

Frenchy stood up and swung a big, empty platter up on one hand. "I go make some more, no?" He looked down at Jerry. "You eat five or six more, hey, boy? They very small."

Jerry attacked the last flapjack on his plate with renewed relish. "A couple more anyway, Frenchy. And maybe another slab of that bacon." He winked as Sandy began to groan. "Who knows, we may get stranded for days in a blizzard without food. I'm storing up energy."

After breakfast, Sandy and Jerry went outside and watched Tagish Charley work out the huskies on the landing strip off to one side of the road station. The dog sled was about ten feet long with a welded aluminum frame and polished steel runners. Extending halfway down both sides, were guard rails to which baggage could be strapped. There was a small footrest at the rear, where the sled driver could ride standing erect, and a rubber-coated handrail for him to grip.

The dogs milled about excitedly as Charley harnessed them to the sled. They were hitched up in staggered formation, one dog's head abreast of the haunches of the dog in front of him. Black Titan led the pack, and the driving reins were attached only to his harness.

"Lead dog, he have to be very smart," Charley told them, ruffling up the thick fur collar around Titan's throat. "He boss of team. Not driver. Other dogs do bad job, he scold them. Sometimes he have to fight a bad dog who make trouble."

"Do you think Professor Crowell's team has a chance to win the race from Whitehorse to Skagway?" Sandy asked him.

"We win," Charley said matter-of-factly. "Best team, best lead dog." He patted Titan's head. "Black Titan pull sled all alone if he have to."

"Is the professor going to drive himself, Charley?" Jerry inquired curiously.

The Indian shrugged his shoulders. "Better he not drive in race. Professor fine dog driver, but safer if he not drive this race. On trail easy for bad men to get him. Better for Charley to drive team."

"Charley," Sandy asked worriedly, "do you have any idea why the bad men are after Professor Crowell? Why would anyone want to harm a nice man like him?"

Anger tightened Charley's features. "Professor

got something they want very bad. They kill him if they have to."

"But *what* do they want? What is it the professor has that's so valuable to them? Money? Jewels?"

Charley shook his head. "Professor no have money or jewels. Maybe something he have in here." He tapped his finger against his forehead wisely.

Sandy looked at Jerry. "You know, he could have something there. I think I'm going to have a man-to-man talk with my dad first chance I get."

The two boys rode on the sled as ballast while Charley put the powerful team through its paces, whizzing back and forth on the hard-packed surface of the landing strip and churning through high drifts in the virgin snow around the fringes.

"Great!" Jerry yelled in Sandy's ear, clutching the guard rail with one hand and, with his other hand, protecting his face from the spray of snow flung back by the dogs' flying feet. "This is better than the roller coaster at Disneyland."

Sandy nodded vigorously. "That Titan is fantastic, isn't he? He acts almost human."

Seemingly aware of his admiring audience, Black Titan put on an impressive display. Setting a pace for his teammates that kept their tongues lolling from their black-roofed mouths, he guided them smoothly into sharp turns and sudden twists and broke trail through muzzle-high snow with his broad chest as if it were light as dust—all the time responsive to the slightest tug at the reins.

"He's a marvel, all right," Sandy told Charley later when the dogs were resting after their work-out.

"Boy, would I ever like to get into that big race. You don't need any passengers, do you, Charley?" Jerry asked.

"Okay for you boys to come along. Need five hundred pounds on sled anyway."

Sandy was overjoyed. "You mean it, Charley? Really? Jerry and I can ride ballast on the sled?"

"Sure. You ask professor."

At that minute, Dr. Steele came walking across the landing strip toward them. "You fellows about ready to leave? It's nine-thirty. Superintendent MacKensie has had our vehicles warming up for almost half an hour now."

Sandy spoke to Jerry in a low voice. "You help Charley get the dogs in the truck. I want to talk to my dad—in private."

CHAPTER FIVE

Christmas in the Wilderness

"DAD," Sandy began haltingly as they walked slowly back to the barracks, "Professor Crowell is in some kind of trouble, isn't he?"

Dr. Steele was evasive. "You mean because of that man who broke into our cabin? What makes you think that had anything to do with the professor?"

Sandy looked earnestly into his father's eyes. "That was no ordinary thief, Dad. He was after something in Professor Crowell's notes and papers." His face became even graver. "Maybe they're after you, too."

Dr. Steele tried to laugh it off, but his mirth was hollow. "Aren't you becoming a little melodramatic, Son?"

"You don't fool me for a minute, Dad. I know that whatever's going on is probably top-secret government business and you can't tell me what it's all about. But I do think it's only fair to tell me whether or not you or the professor or Lou Mayer are in any danger."

Dr. Steele appeared to think it over very carefully. Finally, he sighed. "Yes, I guess you're right. I brought you boys along, so I don't suppose I have any right to keep you completely in the dark. The fact is we *are* in danger—all of us. I had no right to expose you boys—especially Jerry—to this kind of thing, but I thought at first we could deceive *them* into believing that this was just a routine geological survey. I was wrong. They're far too clever." His mouth tightened. "Maybe the best thing to do would be to send you and Jerry back home."

"Dad!" Sandy looked hurt. "Not on your life. If you're in any kind of trouble, I'm sticking with you until you're out of it."

Dr. Steele frowned. "I wish I could tell you more about this, Sandy, but I'm bound by an oath of secrecy. You'll just have to trust me."

"I trust you, Dad."

"As for Jerry James, I think it's only fair for you to tell him what I've told you and let him decide whether he wants to continue on with us."

"I'll ask him," Sandy agreed. "But I know what he's going to say right now."

They were almost at the front door of the barracks now. "One more thing, Dad," Sandy said. "Tagish Charley. I like him an awful lot. You don't think that he—"

"That he's the one who ransacked our cabin last night?" the doctor finished for him. "The same thought flashed through my mind, too. I just can't believe it, though. Charley's been with the professor for years; he's like one of the family. Still—" his face went grim—"we don't really know—and we can't afford to take chances."

Superintendent MacKensie greeted them as they entered the building. "Your wagons are all set to roll," he announced.

Sandy took his friend aside just before they left the station and repeated what his father had said, offering Jerry the choice of going back to Valley View.

"I ought to slug you," the husky, dark-haired boy roared, his black eyes flashing, his square jaw jutting out defiantly, "for even thinking I'd back out on you when you were in trouble! What kind of a guy do you think I am?"

"Take it easy, Buster." Sandy threw his arm

around his friend's shoulders. "I told Dad that's exactly what you would say."

They made good time all that morning, and a little after one o'clock they reached Fort Nelson. Here they ate lunch with the Game Commissioner, an old friend of Professor Crowell's. Later, while the station wagon and truck were being refueled, the boys accompanied Tagish Charley down to the Indian village on the banks of the frozen Nelson River. Charley went straight to the house of the headman in the village, and they talked earnestly and excitedly in an Indian dialect for some time.

On the way back to the truck, he told the boys: "That man know everything go on in province. He say many strangers pass this way. They say they French trappers, but they speak strange tongue and never sell any furs."

"Did he say how many?" Sandy asked.

"Maybe six."

Jerry clapped his mittened hands together. "And there are five of us. Those aren't bad odds."

"In a fair fight," Sandy corrected him. "But from what I've heard and seen of these guys, they probably have no idea of fighting fair."

The sun went down early, but this night was

clear and the sky was full of stars, so they drove on for quite a while after dark. At five-thirty they came to a weather station near Lake Muncho. It was a small place, manned by three technicians, and although the five guests really crowded their quarters, the weathermen were very hospitable.

"You chaps are lucky," the man in charge told them. "This high-pressure area should be with us for the rest of the week. You'll have fine weather all the way to Alaska."

"Gosh," said Jerry, when he saw the small pine tree trimmed with tinsel and colored balls and lights that stood in one corner of the shack's main room. "I almost forgot—this is Christmas Eve."

"It doesn't seem like it, somehow," Sandy said, feeling a slight twinge of homesickness. "Not without Mom's turkey dinner and presents and Christmas carols."

"Christmas isn't turkey and presents and chimes," Professor Crowell observed. "It's what you feel in the heart."

"You're right, sir," Sandy admitted. Then he grinned. "I guess Jerry and I are still kids at heart."

"That's as it should be," the professor said. "It's one of the things I admire most about you Americans—your boyish exuberance. You're al-

ways looking for an excuse to give a party. I think
it's one of the reasons why you have so many na-
tional holidays."

"Nothing shy about us Canadians when it comes
to a party either," one of the weathermen put in.
He turned to his two partners. "Let's show these
Yanks a real Christmas party. What do you say?"

There was a chorus of "ayes."

After a hearty meal of tinned ham, fried potatoes and frozen candied yams, topped off by a
flaming plum pudding, they gathered in a tight
circle about the little fireplace and sipped hot
cider and nibbled marshmallows toasted in the
winking embers. About nine o'clock the weathermen picked up a Canadian Broadcasting Corpora-
tion program of Christmas carols on their short-
wave radio and piped it through a big hi-fi speaker
over the fireplace.

"This is more like it," Jerry sighed contentedly,
stuffing himself with marshmallows and roasted
nuts, staring at the lights twinkling on the Christmas tree and listening to the strains of "Silent
Night."

Dr. Steele grinned mysteriously. "And who
knows, maybe Santa will find you boys even up
here. Better pin up your stockings before you go
to bed."

There were only two extra cots at the weather station, so the boys, Lou Mayer and Tagish Charley bedded down in their sleeping bags around the fireplace. Just before he turned in, Charley fed the dogs and let them run for a while on the deserted highway. Then he penned them in on the big front porch of the weather station.

Sandy fell asleep as soon as his head touched the pillow, and the next thing he knew, sunlight was streaming into his eyes. Yawning, he sat up and looked around. Tagish Charley and Lou Mayer were already up and off somewhere. Only Jerry was still asleep, curled up in his sleeping bag like a hibernating bear.

Sandy's eyes widened as they came to rest on the little Christmas tree in the corner. Beneath it were piled assorted boxes wrapped in gaily colored tissue and tied with tinseled ribbon. He leaned over and shook his friend.

"Hey, Jerry, wake up!"

Jerry snorted and opened his eyes, heavy-lidded with sleep. "Whazza matter?" he mumbled.

Sandy grinned. "Looks like Santa was here while we were asleep. C'mon, get up."

Sandy rolled out of his sleeping bag, put on his trousers, shirt and boots and went over to the tree. Kneeling down, he read the tags on the packages: " 'To Sandy from Dad,' 'To Jerry . . .' Hey! There's something here for everybody."

He looked up and saw his father, Professor Crowell and Lou Mayer standing in the doorway that led into the tiny kitchen. They were all smiling broadly.

"Well, don't just sit there," Dr. Steele said. "Pass them around."

As Sandy had observed, there was something for everyone. An intricate chronometer wrist watch that told the days of the month and even the phases of the moon for Sandy; a candid camera for Jerry; a gold fountain pen for Lou Mayer; and a fine steel hunting knife with a silver inlaid handle for Tagish Charley. Professor Crowell, with genuine Yuletide spirit, gave a set of ivory chessmen he had bought from an Indian at Fort Nelson to the three weathermen. They, in turn, presented the professor and Dr. Steele each with a pair of fine snowshoes.

After they had burned the wrappings in the fire, Sandy remarked rather sadly, "Gee, Dad, now I wish I hadn't left your present back home. But Mom said we'd save all the gifts till we got back."

Dr. Steele put his arm around his son's shoulders. "Sandy, the best present you could ever give me is just being here." He reached for Jerry with his other arm. "That goes for you too, Jerry."

Right after breakfast, they said goodbye to their new friends and headed north again. They drove into Watson Lake, just across the border in Yukon territory, about two o'clock. Watson Lake was one of the largest towns along the Alaska Highway. In addition to a Mountie station and an R.C.A.F. base, there was an airstrip for commercial airlines and accommodations for putting up passengers overnight. They drove straight out to the air force base, where the sentry ushered them through the gate with a snappy salute as soon as Professor Crowell identified himself.

"The old prof really rates in these parts, doesn't he?" Jerry mused, as they drove through the precisely laid-out checkerboard streets past neat log-cabin barracks to the HQ building.

They were even more impressed by the reception the professor received from the Base Commander, an old friend he had worked with in World War II.

"You're just in time for Christmas dinner," the Commander told them happily. "Roast turkey with all the trimmings."

Jerry rubbed his stomach gleefully. "This stands to be the best holiday season of our lives, Sandy. Wherever we go people give us Christmas dinners."

The geologists decided to stop over at Watson Lake and get an early start the next morning for the long, grueling uphill drive over the divide.

"What is the divide?" Jerry asked.

"A high shelf on the continent that determines the direction of water drainage," Dr. Steele explained. "In the case of North America, it's the Rocky Mountains. All the rivers and streams on one side of the Rockies run in a generally easterly direction; on the other side they flow to the west."

"Will we have any trouble driving up those mountains with all this snow and ice?" Sandy inquired of the R.C.A.F. Commander.

"Well, it's a pretty tortuous route," the officer admitted. "But the ascent is fairly gradual. With chains you shouldn't have too much trouble. Of course, if it should snow again, that would be another matter."

"We'll get an early start," Professor Crowell told them. "About six A.M."

CHAPTER SIX

Attack from the Air

IT WAS GRAY and cold when they left Watson Lake on the last leg of their journey on the Alaska Highway.

"At Whitehorse, we'll give the car and truck a rest and take to the air," Dr. Steele explained. "The Canadian government has put a plane at the professor's disposal for as long as we're up here."

But the big attraction at Whitehorse as far as the boys and Tagish Charley were concerned was the big dog-sled race to Skagway.

"The professor says it's okay with him if Jerry and I ride ballast," Sandy informed the Indian. "That's if it's all right with you?"

"Okay by me," Charley said. He glanced sideways at Jerry. "But this boy keep eating so much he get too fat to sit on sled."

Sandy let out a guffaw and Jerry pretended to sulk. "You guys have a nerve," he said. "You both lick your plates cleaner than Black Titan does."

"If Tubby, here, is too much of a load for the huskies," Sandy suggested, "we can always let him run behind the sled."

Suddenly, Charley hunched down and squinted through the windshield. "Plane," he announced curtly.

The boys followed his gaze but could see nothing. "Where?" Sandy asked.

Charley pointed toward a line of snow-capped mountain peaks in the distance surrounded by blue haze. Sandy saw a speck that moved out of sight behind one of the peaks. He couldn't make out what it was.

"Are you sure it wasn't a bird?" he said uncertainly.

"It plane," Charley said firmly.

"Maybe it's from one of the road stations," Jerry suggested.

"I guess so," Sandy said and pushed down a little harder on the accelerator to close the gap between them and the station wagon, which had drawn about a quarter of a mile ahead.

Gradually the road climbed, winding and twist-ing through canyons and hugging mountainsides in hazardous stretches. At one such spot Jerry peered down into the chasm that dropped off steeply on one side and clapped his hands over his eyes.

"I think I'll get out and walk the rest of the way," he groaned.

Sandy's face was grim as he nursed the big truck around the curves, never letting the speedometer needle climb above the 30 on the dial.

Then, without warning, a great throbbing roar bore down on them from the rear. Instinctively, they ducked their heads as it seemed to shatter the roof of the cab. An instant later a plane appeared through the windshield zooming down the road toward the station wagon.

"Yipes!" Jerry exclaimed. "What does he think he's doing?"

"The crazy fool!" Sandy said angrily. "He could have scared us off the highway. Look at him! He can't be more than fifty feet off the ground."

The little ship skimmed over the station wagon and started to climb in a wide arc.

"You think it's a scout plane from one of the road stations?" Jerry said anxiously.

"I don't know," Sandy replied, trying to keep one eye on the road and the other on the circling plane. "It looks as if he's coming back again." Gratefully, he noted that they were approaching a less treacherous section of highway.

Once more they heard the little plane gunning its motor at top speed as it flew up behind them. As it passed over them, a small round hole appeared, as if by magic, at the top of their windshield.

For a moment they were too stunned to react, then Jerry yelled, "They're shooting at us!"

With an unintelligible oath, Tagish Charley whirled in the seat and reached back through the curtain partition into the rear of the truck. "Stop!" he told Sandy as he pulled out his hunting rifle.

As Sandy brought the lumbering vehicle to a skidding halt at the side of the road, he saw that the station wagon had pulled up also, and the three geologists were piling out frantically.

Tagish Charley motioned to a patch of timber about a hundred yards away. "Go—fast." The three of them floundered through knee-deep drifts as the engine roar of the plane built up in their ears.

"Down!" Charley bellowed. "Flat!" As the boys flattened out, the Indian turned, dropped to one knee and threw the rifle to his shoulder. He squeezed off two shots, leading the plane as if it were a wild duck. In return, a fusillade of shots from the plane kicked up the snow all around them.

"Those guys really mean business!" Jerry yelled as they scrambled to their feet and ran for the woods again.

"This is like one of those nightmares where you're being chased by a wild animal and your legs move in slow motion," Sandy gasped, churning through the snow.

They reached the trees just before the plane swooped over them again. Crouching behind a tree bole, Charley emptied his rifle at the retreating ship. A slug splattered the bark just above his head.

This time as the plane climbed, a thin spiral of smoke trailed back from the engine, and the rhythm of the motor was uneven.

Sandy let out a cheer. "You got him, Charley! Good shooting."

Immediately the plane broke off its attack and headed north. Sandy led the way down the road to where the three geologists were standing by the station wagon, watching the ship dwindle to a speck in the distance.

"Are you okay, Dad?" he yelled anxiously. "Anybody hurt?"

"No, just badly frightened," Dr. Steele replied. "How about you fellows?"

"No casualties," Sandy reported breathlessly. "Just a bullet hole in the windshield."

"It seems as if Charley saved the day," Professor Crowell said. He took one of the Indian's big hands in both of his. "I'm glad you decided to come along, my friend."

Charley gave him one of his rare, quick smiles. "Bad men try hurt you—" He paused and drew a finger across his throat.

"Like I said before," Jerry declared, "I'm glad he's on our side."

The Indian cocked his head toward the truck, where the dogs were setting up a raucous clamor. "I go see if huskies okay."

Lou Mayer shivered and hugged his arms tightly around his body. "And to think I could have been a teacher in a nice cozy classroom in some peaceful college in the balmy South instead of shooting it out with enemy agents in the Yukon—" He stopped short and looked guiltily at Dr. Steele. "I'm sorry, sir. That just slipped out."

"That's all right, Lou," Dr. Steele said. "I think by now the boys have a pretty good idea of what we're up against." Sensing the question that was forming in Sandy's mind, he added hastily, "But for the present, at least, that's all we can tell you." As Lou and the professor were getting back into the station wagon, he whispered to his son, "At least this little incident answers our question about Charley, once and for all."

"It sure does," Sandy agreed. "We'll see you later, Dad." He and Jerry turned and trudged back to the truck.

Jerry's voice was small and numb. "Wow! Enemy agents! Wow! Wait till the guys hear about this!"

CHAPTER SEVEN

The Big Race

THEY ROLLED into Whitehorse late that night. The boys were surprised to find a fairly modern city with paved streets, rows of stores and shops and street lamps. As they drove down the main street, festively decorated with wreaths, colored lights and holly, Jerry shook his head.

"Why, it looks pretty much like Valley View."

"They even have bowling alleys," Sandy pointed out. "And neon signs."

Later, as they ate supper in the hotel dining room, Dr. Steele told them about the origin of the city: "Whitehorse was born in the gold rush, when thousands of sourdoughs trekked over the mountains from Alaska and the Pacific ports to seek their fortunes. Whitehorse was sort of a jumping-off place. They ran the rapids to Lake Laberge in anything that would float—barges, rafts, scows—and on down the Yukon River to Dawson. A few of them struck bonanzas, but most of them found only poverty and disillusionment. There's just no way to get rich quick."

"I know you're right, Dr. Steele," Jerry remarked. "Though I was kind of hoping that Sandy and I could strike out north with Professor Crowell's dog team and stake ourselves a claim. That French cook back at the road station even gave me a jar of that sourdough of his to get us started."

Professor Crowell laughed. "Before you boys do anything like that, you had better see how you stand up to the rigors of the trail during the big race to Skagway."

"When do we start?" Jerry asked.

"The day after tomorrow."

Charley gulped down a small roll with one bite. "Tomorrow we give huskies plenty exercise. Not much to eat."

Sandy frowned. "You're going to starve them before the race? Won't it weaken them?"

Charley grunted. "No starve. Huskies can go week without food. They little hungry, they run faster and fight harder."

"What are you, Lou and Professor Crowell going to be doing the rest of this week?" Sandy asked his father as they left the table.

His father thought about it a minute before answering. "Well, tomorrow we thought we'd fly up to Fairbanks and visit the University of Alaska. The president's an old friend of mine. We hope to inspect some of the fossils they've dug up lately. I understand they have some fine specimens on display."

"Gee, I wish we could come with you," Sandy said. "That sounds like interesting stuff."

"Yeah," Jerry agreed. "We kids in the States never get to see things like that."

"Why, that's not so, Jerry," Professor Crowell objected. "Your American museums and universities contain some of the most fascinating specimens of prehistoric beasts that I've ever seen. The last time I visited the American Museum of Natural History in New York I saw the leg of a baby mammoth that was completely intact. It had been preserved for centuries in a glacier, and the museum kept it in a deep freeze."

"The professor's right, Jerry," Sandy admitted. "The trouble with so many of the kids we know is that they're too lazy to use their eyes and their ears—and their legs."

Dr. Steele interrupted. "As a matter of fact, did either of you boys know that Black Bart, the notorious stagecoach bandit, is reputed to have buried a strongbox with $40,000 in gold in the hills back of Stockton?"

"Gosh, no!" Jerry exclaimed. "What do you say, Sandy? Let's go on a treasure hunt next summer. That's practically in our back yard."

Professor Crowell smiled. "That beats digging for gold in the Yukon, I'd say."

"How long will you be in Fairbanks?" Sandy wanted to know.

"Oh, no more than a day," Dr. Steele said. "We want to get back to Skagway to see you fellows come across the finish line in the big race."

"In first place, of course," Jerry added smugly.

"That would be a treat," Professor Crowell said.

"Now I think we should all go up to our rooms and get a good night's sleep," Dr. Steele suggested. "We've had a long, trying day."

"That sounds good to me," Lou Mayer seconded. "It will be a real pleasure to rest my weary bones on an honest-to-goodness bed with a soft mattress."

"You chaps go ahead," said Professor Crowell. "I'm going down the street to the police barracks and report that incident with the plane today."

"Do you really think that's wise?" Dr. Steele asked gravely.

"The chief constable is a reliable man," the professor told him. "He can be depended upon to be discreet. He may have received a report from one of these local airstrips about a small plane making an emergency landing. I don't think those fellows could have traveled too far with their engine smoking like that. If they did land near here, we can put our people on their track."

Dr. Steele nodded. "Good idea. Do you want me to come with you?"

"That won't be necessary," the older man assured him. "I'll take Charley along."

Upstairs, when the boys had bathed and changed into their pajamas, they lay in the dark in the small hotel room they shared and discussed the events of the day.

"What do you think it's all about, anyway?" Jerry wondered. "We know enemy agents are after the professor. But why? It's not like he was an atomic scientist or something. What could they want with a plain old geology professor?"

"I don't know," Sandy said worriedly. "But it must have something to do with our reason for coming up to Alaska. You can bet my dad and the professor didn't make the trip *just* to look at fossils and take soil samples. Well, we'll just have to wait and see."

"Br-r-r," Jerry said, "it's like walking through a haunted house on Halloween Eve. You don't know what to expect. But whatever it is, you know it won't be good." He threw back the covers and got out of bed.

"Hey, where are you going?" Sandy demanded.

Jerry padded across the room barefoot. "I just want to make sure that door is locked."

The day of the big race was bitter cold and the sky was leaden with snow clouds scudding across the mountain peaks around Whitehorse. A huge crowd had gathered at the starting line on the outskirts of the city, and the air rang with merry voices and the yelping of dogs. Sandy and Jerry huddled close to a big bonfire outside the officials' tent while Tagish Charley made a last-minute check of the sled and the dogs' harnesses.

One of the judges came up and spoke to Sandy. "I understand you boys are from the States. What do you think of our big country?"

"It's very exciting, sir," Sandy said.

"And very cold," Jerry added.

The judge laughed. "Wait until you're out on

the trail a few hours. Then you'll know how cold it is. You're riding with Professor Crowell's team, right?"

"Yes, sir. And we're really looking forward to it. This is some big event, isn't it?"

The air was charged with a holiday atmosphere. Men and women were laughing and singing as they sipped from steaming mugs of coffee and tea; and a few were drinking from mugs that Sandy suspected contained even stronger brew.

"The race from Whitehorse is a time-honored ritual," the judge told them. "Back in the old days, the course was even longer. From Dawson to Skagway, almost six hundred miles."

"Good night!" Jerry said. "Those poor dogs must have worn their legs down to the shoulder."

"As a matter of fact," the judge went on, "Klondike Mike Mahoney used to operate a mail and freight route from Skagway to Dawson."

"Who was Klondike Mike Mahoney?" Sandy asked.

"A rather fantastic young man who came to the Yukon during the gold rush and became a living legend." He smiled. "You might say he was our counterpart of your Davy Crockett."

"Hey! What are they doing?" Jerry pointed to a group of Eskimos who were laughing and whooping as they catapulted an Eskimo girl high into the air from a large animal hide stretched taut like a fireman's net.

"That's one of their favorite games," the judge said. "You've probably played something like it at the beach—tossing a boy up in a blanket."

"Yeah," Jerry said. "But not like *that*. She's better than some acrobats I've seen on the stage."

Time after time, the slender Eskimo girl shot into the air, as high as twenty-five feet, like an arrow, never losing her balance. While they were watching her, Tagish Charley joined them by the fire. In his one hand he held a sheet of oiled paper on which were spread a half-dozen cubes that looked like the slabs of chocolate and vanilla ice cream served in ice-cream parlors.

"Eat," Charley said, offering them to the boys.

Sandy took one gingerly. "Looks good. But what is it?"

"*Muk-tuk*," the Indian grunted.

"A Northern delicacy," the judge said with a straight face.

Jerry stuffed one of the cubes into his mouth with gusto. "Say, that's good. Tastes like coconut."

Sandy nibbled at his with more reserve. "It does a little. Maybe a little oilier. What's it made of?"

"Whale skin and blubber," the judge informed him. "The white part is blubber, and the dark is hide."

Jerry gagged momentarily, swallowed his last mouthful, then smiled manfully. "I wish you hadn't said that, sir," he declared. "But it still tastes good."

"You ready now?" Charley asked the boys. "Time for race soon."

They shook hands with the official and followed Charley over to the starting line, where the teams were lining up.

There were eight entries altogether. The dogs were prancing about restlessly in their harnesses like proud race horses, their curved tails waving over their backs. They were charged with excitement and seemed eager to get started. The huskies on opposing teams eyed each other sullenly, baring their long fangs and growling deep in their throats. Occasionally, one would dart out of line and snap at another dog, but there were no fights. Black Titan, like the good lead dog he was, watched his team closely, and whenever one of them became too frisky and pugnacious, he would bark a sharp command. Immediately, the offender would drop his ears and quiet down.

"They act almost human," Sandy said.

"I'll say," Jerry agreed. "That Titan reminds me of Mr. Hall, my math teacher. No horseplay when he's around."

Charley helped the boys arrange themselves in the sled, Sandy in back, with Jerry in front of him, sitting between his legs. "Just like on a toboggan," Sandy observed. They tucked the big robe that covered them around their sides as Charley took his place behind the sled and gripped the handles.

The sharp crack of the starter's pistol split the crisp air and Charley's bellowing "Mush! Yea, huskies, mush!" almost split Sandy's eardrums. The figures lined up on both sides of them blurred rapidly as the sled picked up speed, and wind and snow whipped into their faces. Gripping the handles tightly, Charley matched the pace of the team effortlessly with his long strides.

"He's not going to run all the way, is he?" Jerry yelled to Sandy.

"I guess he wants to give the team the best of it this early in the race. He'll hop on when he gets winded."

But a half hour went by and still the driver's boots pounded behind them in unbroken rhythm. At first the seven teams were bunched pretty close together on the hard-packed trail, then gradually the distance between them widened. Sandy kept glancing back as Charley urged their sled into the lead and finally lost sight of the nearest team as they rounded a hummock and entered a stretch of forest.

"If we keep this pace up, we'll be in Skagway in time for lunch," Jerry said.

The big Indian reined in the dogs when they reached a spot where three separate narrower paths forked off the main trail.

"Which way do we go?" Sandy called to him.

Still breathing as easily as if he had taken a short walk around the block, Charley answered, "All go to Skagway. We take middle trail. More snow, but less up and down." Having made up his mind, Charley shouted to the dogs: "Mush! Mush! Mush, huskies!" And they were off again.

A short time later they left the trail and went skimming down a windswept slope that stretched away into a barren icy plain. Now Charley hopped onto the back of the sled and rode like a Roman charioteer, shouting encouragement to the dogs in Indian. Although there was no broken trail, the sled rode solidly on the surface of the old snow crusted over thickly by the 50-below-zero cold.

"This is really living!" Jerry exulted, his voice trailing off eerily in the slipstream behind the sled. At noon they stopped to rest the dogs in the lee of a rock overhang. Sandy broke out a thermos of steaming coffee and sandwiches, and Charley threw the huskies some chunks of lean dry meat.

"How far do you think we've come so far?" Jerry asked.

Charley shrugged. "Twenty, maybe twenty-five mile."

"Say, that's pretty good." He looked back in the direction they had come from. "Where do you suppose those other guys are?"

Charley finished his sandwich, rumpled up the wax-paper wrapping and set a match to it, warming his hands over the brief torch it created. He motioned to the west. "Some follow other trail. Maybe a few stay just in back of us. Let us break new trail for them. Then when our dogs tired, they fresh and catch us." He cupped one hand to his ear. "Listen!"

The boys held their breaths for a minute, straining to hear. They could just make out the sound of barking dogs floating on the wind in the distance.

"He's right," Jerry said indignantly. "That's a sneaky thing to do."

"No, it's not," Sandy disagreed. "No more than

77

a track man letting another runner set the pace."

"No worry," Charley assured them. "We win anyway."

"What a man you are, Charley." Jerry regarded the big Indian with admiration. "We could use you in the fullback spot on the Valley View football team." He grinned at Sandy. "I bet he could walk down the field with both teams on his back."

Charley squinted up at the sky abruptly. The ceiling seemed even lower and grayer than before. "It snow soon. We better go."

Sandy looked up too. "How can you tell?"

"I know," Charley said somberly. "Bad storm on the way."

"Oh, great!" Jerry said. "What happens if we get caught out in this deep freeze in a blizzard?"

"There are check points every twenty-five miles," Sandy recalled what the professor had told him. "We must be pretty close to one now, Charley. Think we should stop and get a weather report?"

Charley nodded toward the east. "Two, three miles over that way. On main trail. We go there, we lose race. We stop at next post, at halfway mark. Three hours away maybe."

"I guess that's the only thing to do," Sandy agreed. "Well, let's get moving."

78

Ten minutes later, the snow began to come down, fine granular pellets that stung like sand as the rising wind blasted it into their faces. Visibility was reduced to no more than fifty feet. Even the dogs were slowed down. The snow, mixed with the loose surface fluff of previous falls, piled up quickly in drifts. As it dragged at his boots more and more, Charley began to mutter angrily to himself in Indian.

"I don't like it, Sandy," Jerry said uneasily. "We're never going to make that check point before dark."

"At this rate we'll never make it at all," Sandy retorted. "Listen, Jerry, what do you say we get out and trot along with Charley? It's bad enough pulling the sled by itself without our weight too."

"Good idea," Jerry admitted. "Let's give the dogs a break."

Sandy signaled Charley to stop and told him of their plan.

"All right," Charley agreed. "I go up front and break trail."

CHAPTER EIGHT

Lost in a Blizzard

FOR THE NEXT HALF HOUR the boys were able to keep up with the sled. But in the ever-deepening snow, their legs grew heavier and heavier. At last, they lost sight of the sled in the swirling flakes. When Jerry slipped and fell, Sandy cupped his hands to his mouth like a megaphone and yelled: "Charley! Char-r-ley! Wait for us."

Gasping for breath, Jerry struggled up to his hands and knees. "I've had it, Sandy," he gasped. "I can't go any farther."

Sandy helped his friend to get up and supported him with one arm. "C'mon, boy, we can make it. As soon as we catch up with the team you can rest awhile in the sled."

Clutching each other tightly, they staggered forward, trying to follow the tracks of the sled runners. But before they had covered twenty-five feet, the blowing snow had obliterated the trail. Sandy continued on doggedly in the direction he thought the team had taken, dragging Jerry with him. Every few steps he would stop and call: "Char-ley! Char-ley!" But there was no answer— only the moaning of the wind and the hiss of the snow beating against the fabric of their parkas.

Once more Jerry sagged to his knees. "We're lost, pal," he muttered. "Look, I'm exhausted. I can't go a step farther. You go ahead and look for Charley. When you find him, you can come back for me."

"Don't be crazy, Jerry. Our best chance is to stick together. If we keep walking, we're bound to catch up to the team. Once Charley finds we're gone, he'll stop and wait for us."

Jerry's voice cracked. "I can't see my hand in front of my face. We don't even know if we're going in the right direction."

While he was speaking, a low, mournful howl drifted to them on the wind from somewhere on their left. Sandy clutched Jerry's arm. "You hear that?" he said tensely.

Jerry's voice brightened. "That must be the

team. C'mon." With renewed vigor, he veered off in the direction of the howling.

Sandy grabbed him with both hands. "No, wait! It could be a wolf."

Jerry stopped dead. "Oh my gosh!" he murmured. "What are we going to do?"

Sandy dusted the snow that had crusted on his eyebrows with the back of one mitten. "I don't know. I still think we're heading in the right direction. Let's go a little farther. If we don't find Charley and the team soon, we can always head over that way."

The snow was coming down so hard now that every breath was an effort. Sandy felt as if he were being smothered in a sea of white cotton. He stopped as the howling broke out again, in a chorus this time.

"Maybe you're right," he said to Jerry. "That sure sounds like a bunch of dogs."

"Yeah, let's give it a try, anyhow," Jerry pressed.

They were just about to veer off in the direction of the howling when they heard a familiar harsh rumbling directly in front of them. It was the unmistakable growl of a husky.

"Charley!" Sandy called out. "Titan! Black Titan!"

A succession of sharp yelps knifed through the storm. "That's the team all right!" Jerry cried.

Miraculously, their legs seemed to find new strength, and they practically ran the rest of the way through the knee-deep snow. Directly ahead of them, the sled loomed out of the darkness. The dogs, in harness, were seated on their haunches or huddled low in drifts to escape the force of the wind. But Charley was nowhere to be seen.

Jerry sagged against the back of the sled. "Oh my gosh! What happened to him?"

"He must have doubled back to look for us and we didn't see him in the storm." Night had deepened the blinding downfall even more.

There was a tremor in Jerry's voice. "You don't think the wolves got him, Sandy?"

"No, they rarely attack a man. Especially with the dogs here. Besides, Charley had a rifle." He rummaged through the packs on the front of the sled. "It's not here, so he must have taken it with him."

"What do we do now?" Jerry wanted to know. "Go back and try to find Charley?"

"That's the worst thing we could do," Sandy said emphatically. "We'd get lost but good. No, the best thing to do is to wait here until Charley gets back."

Jerry was skeptical. "I'm not sure even an old woodsman like Charley can find his way back in this soup."

"Maybe if we shout to him he'll hear us," Sandy suggested.

For the next ten minutes the boys pitted their voices against the intensity of the raging storm. But even in their own ears their shouts sounded pitifully weak. At last they gave it up.

"It's no use," Sandy said hoarsely. "We'll just have to wait." He crouched down in the lee of the sled.

What seemed like hours passed and still there was no sign of Charley. The boys could feel the cold seeping through their heavy clothing and stiffening their limbs. They were both badly frightened now.

"Sandy," Jerry pleaded, "we just can't sit here and do nothing. We'll freeze to death. My nose and cheeks are numb now."

Sandy fought back the panic that was rising in him too. "If we don't lose our heads, we'll be okay, Jerry. The way it looks now, we're going to have to spend the night here. Tomorrow, they'll have search parties out looking for us. I bet the rest of the contestants are in the same boat we are."

"We'll be stiff as washboards by then," Jerry prophesied. "Frozen wolf food."

"Don't be a nut," Sandy snapped. "Now get up and help me rig up a lean-to."

"A lean-to?" Jerry said wonderingly. "What kind of a lean-to?"

"The kind Charley says the Eskimos build on the trail. They fasten a big hide to the side of the sled that's out of the wind and peg the other side down to the ice, or weight it down. The snow piles up against the far side of the sled, forming a solid windbreak, and you have yourself a cozy little tent."

"We don't have any hides," Jerry said.

"We have that big rug in the sled. C'mon, let's get to work."

While Sandy fastened the robe to the top of the sled's guard rail, Jerry weighted the far side down with a pair of snowshoes he found in the sled and heaped up snow on top of the shoes until they weighted down the robe securely. When they were finished, Sandy scooped the excess snow out from beneath the robe and they had a small lean-to with just enough room in it to shelter two people.

"Well, that's that," Sandy said with satisfaction,

brushing off his mittens. "Now I'll unhitch the dogs while you get our supper ready."

The erection of the lean-to had renewed Jerry's confidence. "What'll you have?" he inquired flippantly. "Roast turkey with chestnut stuffing or a thick steak smothered with onions and a side of French fries?"

Sandy played the game with him. "No, I'm getting sick of that goppy stuff. How about a couple of frozen sandwiches and a thermos of cold coffee?"

"Just what I had in mind," Jerry called to him as he rummaged through the packs on the sled. "Are we going to feed the huskies?"

"Sure, get out some of that meat Charley keeps in that big tin can up front."

The dogs seemed overjoyed to see Sandy. They leaped about him, wagging their tails furiously and barking and whining.

"I bet you guys are hungry," Sandy spoke to them. "Keep calm. Your dinner's coming right up."

When he knelt beside Black Titan to remove his harness, the big lead dog jockeyed obediently into the proper position. As soon as he was free, he nuzzled affectionately against the

86

boy's cheek. "Hey!" Sandy laughed. "That is the coldest nose I ever felt in my life." He ruffled up the thick fur around the husky's throat with his fingers, and was surprised to feel the soothing warmth deep down in the animal's undercoat. "Boy, I wish I had your fur, Titan. No wonder you can sleep in a snow foxhole." He pressed both hands against Titan's body gratefully. "That feels good, old boy."

Jerry came up behind him with the can of dog meat. "And look what else I found." He held out a bulky .45 Colt automatic. "It's fully loaded, too."

The sight of the lethal-looking pistol was reassuring. "Dad must have given it to Charley before we left," Sandy reasoned. "He asked me if I wanted to take a gun along, but I knew Charley had his rifle, so I didn't bother. It's a good thing we have it. Now maybe we can signal to Charley. Fire a few shots in the air to let him know where we are."

"Good idea," Jerry agreed. "And I've got an even better one."

"What's that?"

"Let's send old Titan out to find his buddy. Bet you he can do it."

Sandy was pessimistic. "I don't know if he could pick up Charley's trail in a storm like this, but we can give it a try."

While the dogs were gulping down their food, the boys rummaged through Charley's gear until they found a heavy wool shirt that the Indian had recently worn. When Black Titan had finished eating, Sandy held the shirt under his nose.

"Charley, Charley," he kept repeating. "Go find Charley, Titan." He slapped the husky on the rump. "Go on, Titan!"

Titan began to whine as he sniffed at the shirt. Then he trotted off into the blizzard with his head down. When he had disappeared from sight, Jerry turned to Sandy. "Well, what do we do now?"

"Eat supper and climb into our sleeping bags, I guess. But first I want to fire a couple of shots to see if we can signal Charley."

He took out the heavy automatic and levered a shell into the firing chamber. Pointing it up in the air, he pulled the trigger. The muzzle flash lit up the night briefly like lightning, but the shot was muffled by the wind and thick curtain of snow. The dogs milled around nervously and began to bark. Sandy fired one more shot, then shoved the gun back in the pocket of his parka.

"I bet those shots didn't carry over five hundred

feet. I feel as though we're inside a vacuum. I don't want to waste any more shells until this gale lets up a little. C'mon, let's sack in for the night."

They gathered up the sandwiches, coffee thermos, Coleman stove and sleeping bags and crawled into the lean-to. The blowing snow had sealed up all the cracks and even the openings at either end of the makeshift shelter. Sandy burrowed through a drift at the rear of the sled to form an entrance-way.

"This back end gets less wind," he explained to Jerry.

The interior of the lean-to was cramped, but seated with their backs resting against the sides of the sled and their legs crossed in front of them, they were not too uncomfortable. Sandy pumped up the pressure in the one-burner gasoline stove and lit it. He turned the wick up abnormally high until the pale-blue flame became streaked with yellow and began to smoke slightly. Although this was a waste of fuel and reduced the cooking efficiency of the stove, it provided more light and warmth.

"Say, this is all right," Jerry said, grinning. "It reminds me of the time we went on a Boy Scout camping trip and slept in pup tents."

Sandy grinned. "The only difference was we

were only a ten-minute walk away from home and there was a hot-dog stand across the road from the bivouac area." He took a half-frozen sandwich out of the knapsack and passed it to Jerry. "Be careful you don't break your teeth when you bite into it."

"Thanks, pal." Jerry filled two aluminum canteen cups from the coffee thermos and sipped from one. "It's lukewarm, anyway," he commented.

"I've got an idea," Sandy said. "We can heat the cups on the stove and sit the sandwiches on top of the cup. That way the steam will thaw out the bread."

"Brilliant. If it wasn't so cold, I'd take my hat off to you."

Ten minutes later, they were munching hungrily on a relatively decent meal. Jerry inhaled the steam that was rising from his canteen cup and sighed contentedly. "I know it must be my imagination, but right now I'd say this is the best-tasting chow I ever ate."

Sandy laughed and nodded. "We used to say the same thing about the mickeys we roasted in the corner lot when we were kids. All black with ashes and dirt, but boy, they sure did taste good." He lowered the wick a little on the stove. "It's probably the hot coffee, but I'm beginning to get warm in here."

"What's wrong with being warm?" Jerry protested. "Turn it up as high as it will go."

Sandy frowned. "When you live in frigid temperatures it's safer to feel a little cold than it is to be overheated, because when you cool off, the perspiration will turn to ice on your skin."

"Perspiration!" Jerry gawked incredulously. "Are you kidding?"

"Well, we're not going to take any chances. As soon as we're finished eating, I'm going to turn off the stove altogether."

"Not until I'm snug in my bedroll," Jerry begged.

Sandy looked worried. "Poor Charley. He's not going to be very snug tonight. No bedroll, no food. Gee, I wish I knew what happened to him."

"What makes it worse," Jerry said gloomily, "is that it's our fault. If we hadn't dragged so far behind, he wouldn't have had to go looking for us."

The boys finished their sandwiches and coffee in subdued silence, staring out into the stormy night through the diminishing black hole of the entranceway.

"You know," Sandy said suddenly, "in another hour we'll be snowed in tight inside this lean-to."

Jerry surveyed the drifting snow anxiously. "You're right. Like a tomb. We'll be able to get out, though, won't we?"

Sandy reached over and enlarged the opening with one hand. "Oh, yes. It's as light as powder."

After they had finished eating and wrapped up the garbage, they prepared to bed down for the night. "We'd better do this one at a time," Sandy suggested. "We'd only be in each other's way moving around in here together. I'll go outside until you're all settled. You lie with your head up at the front of the sled. I'll lie the opposite way. That way we'll have more room."

Crawling on hands and knees, Sandy pushed through the drift that was blocking up the opening. A furious blast of bitter cold wind took his breath away as he got to his feet and sent him reeling back from the sled. It was even warmer inside the lean-to than he had realized. He recalled that Tagish Charley had a powerful flashlight in his gear and walked through knee-high snow to the front of the sled to look for it. It would be wise to keep it handy in the lean-to, he decided. He found the light easily and turned it on to see how the dogs were making out. They were all huddled together behind the windbreak of the sled, growling and shifting around restlessly. As the flash beam swept over them, a few cringed and bared their fangs. Their behavior distressed Sandy, who had expected that by now they would all be cozily balled up in holes and snoring peacefully. He skirted around them and walked back to consult with Jerry. Beaming the light on the lean-to, he saw that the snow was mounding it over like an igloo. Once more he had to dig the snow away from the entrance before he could get in.

When he crawled inside, he saw that Jerry was stretched out in his sleeping bag, the hooded cover zipped up tightly around his head. Only his eyes, nose and mouth were showing.

"How's the weather outside?" he asked Sandy.

Sandy shook the snow off his hood. "Same as before. Terrible. The dogs are acting up, too. I'm worried."

"Maybe they're cold."

"I don't think so. They act frightened."

"Me too. We're snowbound in the Yukon. Charley's missing, probably frozen to death in a snowdrift. Our food is about gone. What a mess! I'm scared plenty."

At that moment a long, mournful animal howl rose clearly above the intensity of the wind. Before it trailed off, another howl and still another joined it, forming an eerie chorus.

Jerry snapped upright like a jack-in-the-box, his face drained of blood. "Wolves!"

"And close by," Sandy said grimly.

Outside, the dogs were really setting up an uproar now, snarling and barking frantically.

Despite the seriousness of the situation, Sandy had to smile as he watched his friend struggling to get out of the sleeping bag. In his excitement, Jerry couldn't work the zipper. "Get me out of this strait jacket!" he yelled.

"Take it easy," Sandy said. "In that bag you look like a big fat hot dog with a face."

"Not so loud," Jerry cautioned him. "The wolves might hear you. Just hurry and get me out of here."

Between them they finally got the sleeping bag unzipped, and Jerry rolled out. Sandy took the Army .45 out of his pocket and checked the clip. There were still four shells in it.

"Do we have any more ammunition for that cannon?" Jerry asked anxiously.

"Probably up front in Charley's gear. I'm going up to get it."

"I'm going with you," Jerry said promptly. "One of those wolves might poke his snout in here while you're gone."

They scrambled out into the blizzard and stood

up. Sandy switched on the flashlight and swept it in a wide circle about them. The powerful beam seemed to run into a solid wall of white no more than fifty feet away. He turned it on the dogs, who were setting up such a loud racket that it drowned out the howling of the wolves. The huskies were all on their feet now, standing stiff-legged with their tails curled tightly beneath their bellies. Their lips were drawn back over their teeth, and the thick fur around their necks bristled like porcupine quills. Sandy swung the light in the direction of their gaze, and felt his heart flip and miss a beat. Glowing greenishly through the falling flakes was a circle of eyes. They were there for just an instant and then faded back out of range of the beam.

Jerry gripped Sandy's arm tightly. "There must be a whole pack of 'em. They're just waiting for us to fall asleep and then they'll jump us."

One of the huskies began to slink forward toward the wolves, his belly flattened close to the ground.

"Come back here, boy!" Sandy shouted. "They'll tear him to pieces," he muttered to Jerry. He cocked the automatic and aimed in the direction of the glowing eyes. "I hate to waste ammo like this, but maybe we can scare them off."

He fired three shots. The last shot was answered by a sharp yelp of pain.

"You got one!" Jerry yelled excitedly.

"Shh! Listen!" Sandy said. Above the wailing of the storm they could hear wild snarling and yelping.

"Sounds like they're fighting among themselves," Jerry said.

The commotion ended as abruptly as it had begun, and although Sandy kept searching the darkness with the light for a long time, there was no further sign of the wolves. At last, when the dogs quieted down and curled up in burrows, the boys relaxed.

"I guess the shots did scare them off at that," Sandy decided. "Now let's find that box of ammo in Charley's pack, and then we can go back inside and see if we can get some rest."

"Sleep?" Jerry said. "Are you kidding? Suppose they come back again?"

"The dogs will warn us if they do."

Jerry shivered. "Okay. But I'll take the bed next to the wall, just in case."

The snow had completely blocked the entrance, and they had to shovel energetically to clear it. "Man, it's really warm in here," Jerry said as he crawled into the lean-to.

The snow wall that had built up at the other end of the lean-to and on the sled side was smooth and glistening. "Just like an igloo," Sandy said. As soon as they were inside their sleeping bags, he turned off the Coleman stove.

Jerry sighed as the little hut was plunged into pitch-darkness. "If I didn't know better, I'd think I was back in my little trundle bed in Valley View."

"Go to sleep," Sandy grunted. He was facing the entrance and the automatic was within easy reach in his side pocket. In an emergency, he knew he could fire right through the sleeping bag.

Gradually, his eyes became accustomed to the darkness and he could make out the faint outline of the round doorway. His eyelids grew heavier and the hole grew smaller and smaller. Then he dropped off to sleep.

CHAPTER NINE

Trapped in an Icy Tomb

WHEN SANDY AWOKE, it was still pitch-dark inside the lean-to. He was about to roll over and go back to sleep, but he decided to see what time it was first. He pulled down the zipper of his sleeping bag, fumbled for the flashlight and flicked the switch.

The sudden burst of light woke up Jerry. "Whazza matter?" he mumbled.

"Go back to sleep," Sandy told him. "It's still the middle of the night." He turned the spot on his wrist watch. "What the—" he exclaimed, and sat up, startled. He squinted at the dial again, but there was no mistake. It said 7:30. "That's impossible! It must have stopped!" But he held it up to his ear and heard the steady, rhythmic ticking.

"What's the matter with you?" Jerry, fully awake now, propped himself up on one elbow.

Suddenly, Sandy began to laugh. "Oh, I get it. We're snowed in." He explained to Jerry. "My watch said it was half past seven, but I couldn't believe it because it was so dark in here. It's the snow; it's blocking out the daylight."

"It's really morning?" Jerry said doubtfully. "Well, let's go out and find out." He unzipped his sleeping bag.

Propping the torch up in the snow, Sandy tried to push his head and shoulders through the drift that blocked the entrance. It was like running into a stone wall. "Ouch!" he cried. He dug at the snow with his fingers, but his mittens slid futilely off a surface that was as smooth as a skating rink.

"Well, come on," Jerry said impatiently. "Let's go."

"Door's frozen up," Sandy told him. He sat down and tried to kick through the ice with his feet, but couldn't dent it. He turned to Jerry. "Try your end. This one is plugged up solid."

"So is this end," Jerry reported, after pounding away with his hands and feet for several minutes. "So, we'll go out the side." He grabbed one corner of the robe and tugged it loose from where it was anchored under the snow, while Sandy worked on the other corner. Then they pulled it aside, exposing a smooth, glittering expanse of ice behind it.

Sandy tested it with his fist and whistled. "Like iron."

There was a tremor in Jerry's voice. "What goes on around here? Maybe I wasn't kidding last night when I called this thing a tomb."

"Take it easy," Sandy soothed. "It's only snow."

"Yeah, ice," Jerry repeated. "You ever see them drive trucks across the ice on frozen lakes? I've seen it in newsreels. That ice is pretty rugged stuff."

"You got a knife?" Sandy asked. "I left mine in the sled."

"So did I. Say, let's try to move the sled," Jerry suggested.

They both shoved and pulled at the sled for a long time, but it seemed welded to the spot. At last, Jerry sank down exhausted. "I don't get it. What happened?"

Sandy played the light over the walls of the lean-to. "I can guess. Remember how cozy and warm it got in here last night? Between that stove and the heat from our bodies, I bet the temperature in here was a good fifty degrees higher than it was outside. The heat radiates through the snow, causing it to melt partially. Then it freezes up. That's how the Eskimos harden the walls of their snow houses. They build big bonfires in them."

"Only they don't forget to make doors in 'em," Jerry said grimly. "Another thousand years from now, I can see a couple of geologists like your dad and the professor digging us out. Preserved in a block of ice like that baby mammoth."

"It's no joking matter," Sandy said. "We've got to think of a way to break out of here. One thing, though: they're bound to send out search parties and sooner or later they'll find the sled."

"What makes you think so?" Jerry demanded. "The sled is probably covered with snow by now and this must look like any other part of the landscape. And you don't think those dogs are going to hang around here forever, do you? They've probably run off looking for food already."

Sandy felt his heart begin to race madly. "I never thought of that," he admitted. "Well, it's up to us then. What have we got that we can use as a chipping tool?"

"Only thing I can think of that's metal is the Coleman stove."

"That's no good. No sharp edges."

They were silent for a moment, then Sandy

snapped his fingers. "I've got it! The gun!" He took the bulky .45 out of his pocket and held it up in the light. "We'll blast our way out."

Jerry looked worried. "You know what they say about shooting fish in a rain barrel? Well, if one of those slugs ever ricochets inside here, we'll be dead fish."

"It's our only chance," Sandy said. He loaded the gun, cocked the hammer and nudged off the safety with his thumb. Holding the gun at arm's length away from him, he pointed the muzzle at the end where the entrance had been. "Better make sure your hood is pulled tight over your ears," he advised Jerry.

"I'm all set. Let 'er go."

Sandy shut his eyes and tightened his finger on the trigger. The explosion reverberated like a bomb in the small lean-to. Sandy felt the shock wave slam into his face, and the recoil almost tore the gun out of his hand. He sat there stunned for a while.

Jerry's voice screaming in his ear brought him out of it. "Sandy, it worked!"

He opened his eyes to the most wonderful sight he had ever seen. A beam of sunlight was pouring through an opening in the ice wall. The potent, snub-nosed .45 slug had blasted a hole almost four inches in diameter. In the light of the flashlight, he also observed that the ice around the hole was shattered and veined from the shock wave.

Dropping the gun back into his pocket, Sandy got on his knees and began to work on the opening with his hands. Snow and ice crumbled easily, and before long he had enlarged the hole so that he was able to squirm through. Jerry was right behind him. Painfully, they stood up.

"Oh," Jerry groaned. "I feel like a dog on its hind legs." Looking up at the clear blue sky, he threw kisses into the air with both hands. "Mr. Sun, I never figured we'd ever see you again."

It was a perfect, cloudless day without even a breeze. Looking around him, Sandy realized that the high winds of the night before had exaggerated the intensity of the blizzard. Except where it had drifted around the sled and lean-to, no more than twelve inches of new snow had fallen. He discovered, too, that they had been traveling along the ridge of a low hill and had stopped on the most exposed spot in all the surrounding terrain. On either side, the ground sloped away gently into protected valleys thick with fir trees.

After spending hours shut up in the gloom of the lean-to, the boys found the sunlight on the snow blinding. They dug their smoked glasses out of their packs and put them on. The dogs crowded around them, yelping and wagging their tails.

"I guess they're hungry," Sandy said. "Is there any meat left?"

"A little," Jerry said. He went to get the can of food from the front of the sled. As he threw the last chunks of raw horse meat to the huskies, he eyed it forlornly. "I'm so hungry I could eat it myself."

Sandy grinned. "Even some of that *muk-tuk* would look good to me now."

"Are the sandwiches all gone?"

"We finished them last night."

They had just finished feeding the dogs when a faint "Ha-lo-oo-oo . . ." floated through the still air. On a distant ridge the figure of a man and a dog were silhouetted against the sky.

"It's Charley and Titan!" the boys yelled in unison. They began to leap up and down, waving their arms and screaming, "Charley! Over here!"

Less than a quarter of an hour later, the Indian came plowing up the hill with Black Titan floundering behind him. They hugged him joyfully and pounded his back, and even Charley was grinning from ear to ear. He listened solemnly while they related their harrowing experiences with the wolves and how they had been trapped in the lean-to.

Charley had had a pretty bad time of it himself. He admitted that, for the first time in his life, he had lost his way when he went back to look for the boys, and had somehow mistaken east for west. Confused and blinded by the shifting gale winds and whipping snow, he had wandered off to an adjacent ridge. After walking around for hours, he had become exhausted—he had been tired out by running twenty-five miles behind the sled to start with—and erected a lean-to in a clump of thick pine trees in the sheltered valley. He had built a big fire and had fallen asleep beside it almost immediately. The next thing he knew, Black Titan was licking his face and the first streaks of dawn were filtering through the pine branches overhead. He had been searching for the boys when he heard the gunshot.

Using the snowshoes as shovels, the three of them dug the sled out of the snow bank. The intense heat of the sun softened the hard upper crust and melted the ice that had formed around the runners. Then Charley hitched up the dogs and headed for the nearest check point, which was only a few miles away.

Their arrival created quite a bit of excitement. "Only one other sled has come through here," a worried official told them. "The Mounties have planes and search parties out looking for the others."

"We saw one of the planes," Sandy said. "He dipped his wings and we waved to him. So he knew we were all right."

"Actually, though," the official went on, "the storm looked worse last night than it was. Those winds were gale force. I don't imagine anyone was really in serious trouble. They're all experienced woodsmen, accustomed to roughing it on the trail."

Jerry hooked his thumbs inside his belt and puffed out his chest. "Sure, it was a breeze."

Tagish Charley was more interested in the sled that had passed through the check point that morning. The official said the other driver had about one hour's start on them.

"We catch 'im," Charley said. "Let's go."

"Hey!" Jerry complained. "What about breakfast? I'm so ravenous, I'm liable to take a bite out of one of the dogs."

"No time to eat," the Indian said. "We have to win race."

"We'll give you some sandwiches and hot coffee

to take along," the official promised. "You can eat on the run."

Jerry stared wistfully at the platters of flap-jacks, juicy Canadian bacon and hot biscuits on the stove. "If we come out of this alive, I'll never look at a cold sandwich again," he vowed.

A short time later, they were racing down the trail. It was a good day, and by nightfall they had covered another forty-five miles and overtaken the sled ahead of them. Its driver turned out to be a young uranium prospector. For five years he and his brother had been competing in the big race. Two years before, they had come in first and they were hoping to repeat this year. They were pleasant young men and spent the night with Charley and the boys at the last check point on the route.

That night, after a hearty supper, they sat around the fire talking to Sandy and Jerry. Tagish Charley went to bed as soon as he had the team fed and settled in the barn. About nine o'clock, another sled arrived at the check point, and the driver reported that still another team was camped at the side of the trail about an hour's ride away.

"This is really going to be a photo finish," one of the brothers said. He got to his feet and knocked the ash out of his pipe into the fireplace.

"We better sack in, men. There's going to be a mad scramble to get away first in the morning."

Sandy and Jerry followed them to the big dormitory bedroom, where a dozen army cots were set up around a potbellied stove that glowed a dull cherry-red in the darkness. Charley was already snoring loudly as they slipped into their bedrolls.

"Now how are we supposed to get to sleep with that big lug sawing wood?" Jerry grumbled. "We may as well sit and . . . and . . . talk . . . around . . . the . . . fire . . ." His voice trailed off into a pretty good imitation of a buzz saw of its own.

CHAPTER TEN

Down the Chilkoot Chute to Victory

IT SEEMED TO SANDY that he had just closed his eyes when he felt rough hands on his shoulders, shaking him. "Time to go," Charley's voice whispered.

"What time is it?" he mumbled, raising himself on his elbows.

"Four o'clock," Charley said. "Other fellers hitching up already."

Sandy struggled out of his sleeping bag and sat on the edge of the cot, stretching. It was still dark, but when Charley opened the stove door to throw on another log, he could see that the cots that the two brothers had slept on were empty. Yawning, he raised his left foot and kicked the cot where Jerry was still sleeping soundly.

"Rise and shine!" he called to his friend.

They ate a hurried breakfast of hot cereal and scalding coffee, and by four-thirty they were on the trail again. The cold wind in their faces and the stinging spray kicked up by the dogs' feet brought them fully awake before they had gone far.

When it began to get light, the boys got out of the sled and trotted along with Charley. They kept it up for a mile or so before Jerry developed a bad case of rubber legs and went down on his knees.

"I feel like a dope," he said, as Sandy helped him back into the sled. "Here we are, a couple of kids, puffing like steam engines, and an old guy like Charley isn't breathing any harder than if he had run up a flight of stairs."

"And we're in pretty good condition from being in school athletics. Can you imagine how some of the other guys in school would make out?" Sandy asked. "The guys who hop in the family car to go down to the corner newsstand and sneak smokes between every class?"

"Yeah," Jerry agreed ruefully. "The kids in the States are getting soft, there's no doubt about it."

"My Uncle Russ always says you should take at least as much pride in your body as you do in your home. Most people wouldn't live in sloppy, run-down houses, but a lot of them don't care if they spend their lives in sloppy, rundown bodies."

Jerry slapped his middle irritably. "Let me tell you, I'm going to work on this flab when I get home. Old Charley here has taught me a lesson. You miss a lot of the fun of life if you're out of shape."

Sandy kept up with Charley for another mile, then he got back into the sled. He noticed that the Indian held to a pattern: he would run along for a half hour or so and then hitch a ride on the sled for ten minutes. It seemed as if he could go on like that endlessly and tirelessly.

They stopped at mid-morning to give the dogs a rest and brew some strong Indian tea. Charley wouldn't drink the coffee in the thermos. "Coffee no good. You ever see huskies drink coffee?" The boys had to admit that they never had. "Indian tea like medicine. Make you strong and healthy. Dogs know." To demonstrate, he poured a little into a tin plate for Titan, and the big lead dog lapped it up promptly.

"It sure doesn't look as if we're ever going to catch those guys ahead of us, Charley," Sandy commented, dropping a handful of snow into his cup to cool it.

Charley looked down the trail behind them. "They behind us now. Last hill we pass, we go around the long way, maybe mile longer. They go through valley."

Jerry blinked. "If we came the long way, how come we're ahead of them?"

The Indian shrugged. "That valley like pocket after big snow. Drifts three, four feet deep. They have plenty trouble getting through."

Sandy grinned. "What a sly old fox you are, Charley."

They were traveling high in the coastal mountains of British Columbia now, moving through the Chilkoot Pass. Just before noon, they arrived at a customs check point.

"You're the first team through," the mounted policeman who waved them past shouted.

Abruptly, the trail appeared to end at the edge of a cliff. Charley reined the team in and motioned for the boys to step to the rim of the drop-off. Here they saw that, in reality, the trail continued on down a steep incline that resembled the big drop on a roller coaster. For almost 1,200 feet it fell away at a 45-degree angle into the coastal valley below. It was a magnificent spectacle.

Jerry gulped hard. "We're not going down *that* in a sled, are we?"

Tagish Charley nodded curtly. "Chilkoot Chute. We take dogs off first. They follow us down." He walked back and began to remove Black Titan's harness.

Sandy grinned at Jerry. "You ever been on a bobsled?" Jerry shook his head mutely. "Well, after this it'll be a cinch."

When the dogs were unhitched, the boys climbed aboard the sled, and Charley pushed it to the edge of the chute. It teetered briefly, then nosed down the incline.

"Alaska next stop!" Sandy yelled as they picked up speed. A rush of air choked the words off in his mouth, and his stomach rose up in his rib cage with a sickening sensation that was ten times worse than he had ever experienced in an elevator.

Faster and faster the sled shot down the slope, swaying from side to side, as Charley, riding the tail, shifted his weight skillfully to steer it. Behind it the dogs skidded and scrambled down the chute, barking and yelping excitedly. The sled reached the bottom and glided down the trail almost half a mile before it came to a halt.

"What a ride!" Jerry exclaimed.

"We must have skidded halfway to Skagway," Sandy said. He got out of the sled and looked back at the Chilkoot Chute. "Gee, it doesn't look so bad from here, but when you're on it, you'd swear it was a perpendicular wall."

The dogs finally caught up and Charley hitched them to the sled again. "We win now easy," he said matter-of-factly.

As they approached Skagway, they passed cabins, farms and other signs of civilization. A group of children playing in one yard gave them a lusty cheer and chased after the sled. Farther along, other children tagged on to the caravan along with three dogs.

Then, up ahead on the outskirts of the city, they saw a big crowd of people. "Finish line," Charley informed them.

When the sled came into view, a tremendous roar went up and continued unabated as they shot past a man waving a flag. The next thing Sandy knew, they were engulfed by a sea of well-wishers, and men were pounding him on the back so enthusiastically that it took his breath away. At last he spied his father and Professor Crowell fighting their way through the throng.

"Dad!" he called out happily. "We made it."

Dr. Steele reached the boys and threw an arm

around each of them. "Congratulations! This was quite a race, I hear."

"Charley is the guy who rates the congratulations," Sandy answered.

Professor Crowell pounded Tagish Charley on the back ecstatically. "I'm the proudest and happiest man in the world. I haven't felt like this since my twin girls were born. Thank you, Charley."

Charley knelt down and put his arms around Black Titan, who was accepting praise and pats from all quarters with the dignified reserve of a true champion. "Dogs win the race. Charley just come along for ride."

Later, back at the hotel, after a warm bath and a good supper, the boys recounted the adventures they had had during the race.

"Bless my soul," Professor Crowell said to Jerry, "now you really have an idea of the rigorous life that the sourdoughs led. Does it still sound appealing to you?"

Jerry forked the last piece of homemade apple pie from his plate. "I've come to the conclusion that I'm just a city boy at heart, sir," he declared emphatically.

"How was your visit to Fairbanks?" Sandy asked his father.

"We had a fine time," Dr. Steele said. "I gathered some priceless material for the pamphlet I'm preparing on the Pleistocene Era." He smiled. "But promise you won't tell Quiz Taylor, Sandy."

Sandy laughed. "I know what you mean, Dad. My solemn word, I won't mention it."

"What's on the agenda now, Dr. Steele?" Jerry inquired. "Are we going home?"

"Not for another few days, Jerry," Dr. Steele said. "The professor and I want to fly up to Valdez and look over some old mining sites."

"Where's Valdez?" Jerry asked.

"The most northerly ice-free port in Alaska. It used to be the shipping point for copper ore until the Kennecott mines closed down in 1938. We had planned an exciting outing for you fellows—" he hesitated and looked wryly at Jerry—"but inasmuch as Jerry says he's a city boy at heart, well, maybe we'd better forget it."

"What kind of an outing, Dad?" Sandy asked.

Dr. Steele lit his pipe and blew a cloud of smoke at the ceiling. "We won't be using the plane for several days, and we thought you might like to visit Kodiak Island. One of the instructors from the university will be spending a week there, hunting bear, and he said you boys would be welcome to join him." He winked at Sandy. "But I'm not sure your city friend here would be up to it."

"That's all right," Sandy said. "Jerry can stay here at the hotel until we come back."

"Not on your life!" Jerry snorted. "I want to take one of those bearskins back to my mom."

Tagish Charley looked up from his plate solemnly. "Kodiak bear plenty bad killer. Maybe he take your skin back to his mamma."

Everyone except Charley laughed.

The next morning they boarded the big Norseman plane and headed northwest up the coast for Valdez. As they flew over the glacier-ribbed mountains, the boys were awed by the wild beauty of the country beneath them.

"It's so primitive," Sandy remarked. "I don't think man will ever tame it."

"Yes, he will," Dr. Steele said. "As surely as he tamed the American West. We just didn't pay much attention to it until after World War Two."

"A land of untold riches," Lou Mayer mused. "Gold, copper, silver, coal, lead, tin, mercury, platinum—Lord knows what else." He looked over meaningfully at Dr. Steele.

"Things are certainly moving fast," Dr. Steele

went on, a little too quickly, Sandy thought. "Oh, yes, Son, in another fifty years Alaska will be as civilized as California."

"But not nearly so warm," Lou Mayer added.

Professor Crowell smiled. "I don't know, I like our northern winters. They make for greater intimacy among families and friends. When the temperature is fifty below zero and the snow is piled up to your window sills, there is literally no place like home. You discover that being together in front of a warm fireplace can be just as enjoyable as running off to the theater, bridge clubs, night clubs, bowling alleys and all your so-called civilized diversions. The trouble with so many young people these days is that they try too hard to have fun."

Jerry scratched his head thoughtfully. "Professor, you know, you're right. I can't think of any time in my life when I've had more fun than I did the Christmas Eve we spent at that little weather station."

Dr. Steele took out a small wallet calendar and consulted it. "Which reminds me that tonight is New Year's Eve."

"Isn't it funny how you keep forgetting about the holidays up here?" Sandy said. "I guess they see the old year out pretty quietly. Not like the States."

Professor Crowell's eyes twinkled through his glasses. "Don't bet on it, son. Some of the New Year's parties I've been to in the North make your Stateside celebrations seem like pink teas. In the old days, I remember some shindigs that went on continuously from Christmas right through New Year's." He smiled nostalgically. "I wouldn't be surprised if a few of them were still going on."

"But we'll be spending our New Year's on Kodiak," Jerry reminded them. "I was looking at it on the map. It's just a dinky little island."

"Not so dinky," Dr. Steele said. "It's about a hundred miles long, you know. And I think you'll find that its citizens have just as much holiday spirit as the people in the States."

"Do many people live on Kodiak?" Sandy asked.

"It's not too heavily populated," Dr. Steele admitted. "Once it was the center of the Alaskan fur trade. The Russians settled in the town of Kodiak in 1784, and it wasn't until much later that they moved their headquarters to the mainland.

"Nowadays it's hard to make a living on Kodiak. I think the only major occupation is salmon fishing. There's rich farming land at the south end of the island, but the natives have always had difficulty raising sheep and cattle. Too many hungry bears around."

Jerry squinted down the barrel of an imaginary rifle. "Well, there'll be a few less after we get there, eh, Sandy boy?"

Tagish Charley, who had been staring moodily out of the window, turned his quizzical black eyes on Jerry. "You shoot big as you talk, everything be fine."

"I think you better go along and take care of these fellows, Charley," the professor suggested.

"That would be great," Sandy said. "How about it?"

Charley appeared to consider the proposition for a moment, then looked gravely at Sandy from beneath his black eyebrows. "Charley like to go to Kodiak. But better not. I stay and look out for professor."

CHAPTER ELEVEN

Off to Hunt Kodiak Bears

AT QUARTER AFTER TWELVE the Norseman put
down on the outskirts of Cordova, and the three
geologists disembarked along with Tagish Charley.

"You'll be in Kodiak before dark," Dr. Steele
told the boys before he left them. "The pilot will
radio ahead so Professor Stern can be on hand to
meet you when you land. Be sure and bring us
back a bearskin."

"We will," Sandy promised. "And we'll see you
back here on the third of January."

"Goodbye, Doctor," Jerry said. "And Happy
New Year."

"Thank you, Jerry, and the same to you." Dr.

Steele winked. "Don't eat too much *muk-tuk*."

As soon as the plane was refueled, they took off again. When Jerry began to nod drowsily, Sandy went up front and sat down in the copilot's seat.

Russell Parker, the pilot, was a chunky, gray-haired man in his late forties, a veteran of the World War II Air Corps. "I was stationed in the Aleutians for four years," he told Sandy. "The place sort of grew on me. There was this girl in Anchorage, too. Well, as soon as the war was over we were married, and I decided to settle here permanently. I had no family ties back in the States, so the transition was easy." He smiled. "You might say I found a home here."

"And you've been a bush pilot ever since?" Sandy said. "Boy, that must be an exciting life."

"Well, I wouldn't call it exciting exactly. A little romantic maybe—everything about *Alashka* is romantic."

"*Alashka?*" Sandy looked puzzled. "I notice you always say it that way."

"It's an ancient Aleutian term. Means the 'big land.' "

"It's big all right," Sandy said, glancing out of the cockpit window. Below the plane, twin mountain peaks reached up through the wispy clouds. Cupped in the valley between them lay a gigantic glacier whose front was a solid wall of ice ten miles across and as high as a fifteen-story building.

"That's why there are plenty of jobs for bush pilots," Parker explained. "We're like taxi drivers back in the States. To get around in the big land you have to take giant steps. A quick trip to the city may mean a hop of a hundred miles or more. You should see Lake Hood on a Saturday morning in the summer—that's in Anchorage, my home town. Hundreds of little planes."

"It looks like a supermarket parking lot," Sandy finished the thought for him. "Professor Crowell told us."

"It's worse. More like Times Square in New York."

"But since so many people up here have their own planes, doesn't it cut down on your jobs?" Sandy wanted to know.

"Not really. Most of the amateurs are pretty cautious, as they should be. They'll only fly in perfect weather, and stick to the safe air routes. When there's a tough job to be done in a hurry, they call on a bush pilot. I've carried everything from heavy machinery to medical supplies. I've been a flying ambulance, too; I don't know how many lives I've helped to save in the back country."

"Do you often get assignments like this one?" Sandy asked.

"I've flown my share of VIPs, but mostly it's a job for military pilots."

"You consider my dad and Professor Crowell VIPs?"

"I got that impression," Parker said guardedly. He was about to add something else when a burst of static from the radio diverted his attention. "Tower at Anchorage calling us," he told Sandy, adjusting his earphones. He listened, then flipped the switch over to transmit. "N-140 to Anchorage . . . Read you clear . . . Climbing to 12,000 feet . . . Over and out." He flipped the switch and reported to Sandy. "We're climbing another 4,000 feet. We're heading into a snow squall off Kodiak, moving northeast."

Jerry awoke from his nap and came up front to join them. "You guys hungry? I'm going to break out the sandwiches."

Sandy laughed. "Is eating all you ever think about?"

Jerry flicked Sandy's cowlick with one finger. "Especially when I ride in airplanes. I have to keep my stomach weighted down so it won't do flip-flops."

"Okay, I'll join you," Sandy agreed. "How about you, Mr. Parker?"

"I'll wait awhile," the pilot declined. "Soon as we level off at 12,000, I'll set her on automatic pilot."

The boys walked back to their seats and opened the lunchbox the hotel had prepared for them that morning.

"I was just thinking," Jerry said, chewing on a chicken leg, "we haven't seen anything of those characters who took pot shots at us for a few days now. Think they've given up?"

Sandy's brow furrowed in anxiety. "I don't know, Jerry. From what we know of them, they don't seem to be the kind who give up so easily. They've been after the professor for months now. Maybe we should have stayed with them back at Cordova."

"Aw, what could happen to them in Cordova? Those birds wouldn't try anything in the middle of a big town like that."

Sandy nibbled at his sandwich without relish. "I suppose not. But Dad and the professor are going to be out poking around some old abandoned mine sites."

The discussion ended when Parker called back,

"I'm ready for that sandwich now. And a cup of coffee if you don't mind. Black, no sugar."

"I'll take it up to him," Jerry said.

It was still bright daylight in the air when they sighted Kodiak, but the island and the sea around it were shrouded in purple dusk. Lights began to twinkle on below as they circled the city of Kodiak, losing altitude. Towering prominently over the other low buildings were a pair of onion-shaped domes.

"What's that?" Sandy asked Parker. "They look almost Turkish."

"The Russian Orthodox church," the pilot said. "Remember, the Russians founded Kodiak."

"How did those Russians ever get way over here?" Jerry wanted to know.

"Boy, are you dumb!" Sandy said. "On the west side only a thin strip of water separates Alaska from Russia. The Bering Strait is only about forty miles wide."

Parker nodded. "In the winter you can cross it on a sled."

That thought seemed to sober Jerry.

Parker touched the Norseman down gently on its skis and reversed the propeller to brake their slide. As they climbed out of the plane, the figure of a man emerged out of the glare of the landing lights. Clad in fur trousers, fur hood and fur parka, he looked like an Eskimo. But as he approached, Sandy could make out a small clipped mustache and rimless eyeglasses.

"Welcome to Kodiak," he greeted them. "You must be Dr. Steele's son." He held out his hand.

"Yes, sir." Sandy smiled. "I'm Sandy."

"I'm Kenneth Stern."

Sandy performed introductions all around. It turned out that Parker and the young university teacher were friends. "My wife took some courses with Professor Stern," the pilot explained.

Stern clapped his fur mittens together. "I have my jeep parked over at the edge of the field. Let's get back to the lodge. Dora—that's my wife—has a big bear roast in the oven. I imagine you fellows are pretty hungry."

"You go ahead," Parker said. "I want to make sure they put my baby safely to bed. I'll hitch a ride to your camp."

"All right, Russ," Stern said. "We'll hold supper for you."

"What's he got to do?" Jerry inquired as they walked through the crunchy snow to the jeep, which was almost hidden by the great cloud of smoke that was pouring out of the exhaust.

"He wants to make sure the crankcase gets drained," Stern said. "You really do have to treat machinery as if it were a baby in cold like this. That's why I left the jeep running. It could freeze up in a few minutes."

As they drove through the town of Kodiak, the boys were fascinated by the atmosphere. The cultures of three centuries and varied races were blended startlingly but not offensively.

"It's like being on a Hollywood sound stage where the sets are all mixed up," Sandy said breathlessly.

"Mostly, it reminds me of the Old West," Jerry said. "Dodge City. I almost expect to see Wyatt Earp come striding down the middle of the street with his hands on his six-guns."

Professor Stern laughed. "That's an apt description, Jerry. This is the twentieth-century American frontier in a sense. It's only fitting that the characteristics of the frontier should predominate."

The hunting lodge was a sprawling two-story log building about a mile outside of Kodiak, with a wide porch running around it on three sides. Lights blazed warmly from its windows as they pulled in the drive and bumped along to a big barn at the back of the house.

"Four other teachers and myself own it jointly," Stern explained. "We bought it about ten years ago as a summer place. The fact is, we've been using it just as much in the winter as a hunting lodge."

"Did I understand you to say we were having bear roast for supper, Professor?" Jerry inquired politely.

"Yes. You're not squeamish about eating it, are you?"

"Uh, no!" Jerry assured him. "After some of the things I've been eating since I came to Alaska, bear sounds like steak to me."

"It's better," Stern told him. "You wait and see."

"Did you shoot the bear, sir?" Sandy asked.

"No, we haven't been out yet. This is a piece of meat we've had in the freezer since last year."

Jerry laughed. "You're kidding. What do you need a freezer for up here?"

"That's where you're wrong, young fellow. It so happens that the old joke about selling iceboxes to Eskimos isn't such a joke any more. During the war, the Army discovered it was a lot more practical to keep food in freezers than it was to stow it in a shed outside. You see, the temperature drops to sixty and seventy below zero some nights in this country. That's about forty to fifty degrees lower than the coldest deep freeze. At that temperature food takes hours to thaw out. In the freezer, it keeps just right."

Jerry shook his head. "Can you beat that! Next thing you know, the Arabs on the Sahara desert will be turning to steam heat."

They followed Stern along a path to the back door of the lodge. Mrs. Stern, a young woman in ski pants and sweater, was in the kitchen basting the roast when they came in. "Supper will be another hour yet," she apologized. "I hope you boys can hold out."

"That's good," Stern said. "Russ Parker will be along later." He turned to the boys. "Come on inside and meet Chris Hanson and his wife. They'll be spending a few days with us too."

"Chris Hanson?" Sandy repeated it thoughtfully. "There used to be an All-American tackle by that name."

Stern grinned. "That's our boy. He's an athletic coach at the university."

"Say, that's great!" Jerry exclaimed. "Chris was the best." Self-importantly, he added, "As a matter of fact we have a lot in common. I expect to make All-American tackle myself some day."

Sandy smirked and dug his fist playfully into

Jerry's midsection. "You get any fatter, you won't be able to bend down to flip the ball."

Chris Hanson was a brawny man who made even a six-footer like Sandy Steele feel like a little boy. He reminded Sandy of the paintings of fierce Vikings he had seen in grade-school history books, though his blond hair was a bit thin on top. His wife was a small, thin woman who sat as close to the fire as possible, despite the fact that she was bundled up in sweaters. The Hansons were just finishing a game of Scrabble when the boys arrived.

"I'm a Georgia girl, you know," Mrs. Hanson said in a marked Southern accent. "And I don't believe I'll ever get used to this climate."

"We have a friend who would sympathize with you," Sandy told her. "Lou Mayer, my father's assistant."

Chris grinned devilishly. "Oh sure, we met Lou when your dad came up to Fairbanks. Took him skiing once. I don't think he likes me very much."

While they waited for supper to be served, the boys coaxed Chris to reminisce about some of his big gridiron games. Hungry as they were, it was an unwelcome interruption when Mrs. Stern announced: "Chow's on the table."

There were seven people at the table—including Russ Parker, who arrived just as they were sitting down—and among them they picked an eight-pound sirloin bear steak clean.

Jerry swabbed his plate clean with a crust of bread. "That was delicious, Mrs. Stern."

"That's an understatement," Sandy said, "considering that you had three portions."

"I know I made a hog of myself," Jerry admitted. "But when I bag one of those big Kodiaks tomorrow, you can fill up your freezer with steaks."

Mrs. Stern smiled. "That's very thoughtful of you, Jerry."

Chris Hanson looked amused. "You ever done any hunting before, Jerry?"

"No, but I'm on the high-school rifle team back home."

Sandy winked at Chris. "He's the guy they're talking about when they say, 'He couldn't hit the side of a barn.'"

Jerry reddened as everyone laughed, and glared at Sandy. "I suppose you think you're Davy Crockett?"

"Seriously, though," Professor Stern interjected, "a bear hunt can be very dangerous. Some of these brutes on Kodiak are virtually indestructible. And when they're wounded—well, just watch out. There's an old saying among hunters that you've got to kill a Kodiak with your first shot, or you never will kill him. I've heard men who have stalked lions, tigers—all kinds of big game—concede that a Kodiak is the most fearsome of all beasts."

"On second thought," Jerry said gravely, "maybe I'll just stay back here and play Scrabble with the ladies."

After supper the boys cornered Chris Hanson again and discussed football and other sports. At ten o'clock, Professor Stern drove Russ Parker into town.

"Some of the boys invited me to a party at the airport," Russ explained. "I hate to run away like this, but my brother-in-law is going to be there. I haven't seen him in a while. He's in the service, stationed in the Aleutians."

"That's perfectly all right," Mrs. Stern said.

"You don't fool us, Russ," Chris Hanson kidded him. "You just want to sneak out of that bear hunt tomorrow."

Parker snorted. "You aren't going to drag me off after any bears. Not unless I can hunt them from the air."

"When are we going back to Cordova, Mr. Parker?" Sandy asked him.

"I figure you can have a couple of days of hunting. The professor expects us back on the third of January."

Professor Stern asked the boys whether they wanted to ride into town with him and see how the Kodiakans celebrated the New Year, but they declined.

"We heard they had some pretty wild times up here," Jerry said. "But the way I feel, the only thing that would look good to me is a soft, warm bed."

And by twelve o'clock they were in bed. "I wonder what the gang is doing back in Valley View," Jerry sighed as they lay in the dark listening to the sound of foghorns in St. Paul's harbor blending with church bells and firecrackers in distant Kodiak.

"You can bet they're not planning to go bear hunting at six in the morning," Sandy answered sleepily.

CHAPTER TWELVE

Treed by a Wounded Bear

PROFESSOR STERN roused the boys at eight o'clock on New Year's morning. "Put on two suits of long woolen underwear and two pairs of socks," he instructed them. "We'll probably be out until dark."

They dressed quickly and went downstairs to the big kitchen, where Chris Hanson was cooking breakfast. "How'll you have your eggs, fellows?" he asked.

"Sunny side up," Sandy answered. "Can we help?"

"Sure. You can start the toast."

Sandy took a handful of sliced bread out of the bread box and began searching through the cupboards. "Where's the toaster?" he asked finally.

Chris smiled and pointed to the stove. "Right here. Just butter the bread lightly and spread the slices out between the lids."

For the first time, Sandy became aware that the cooking stove was the old-fashioned, cast iron, wood-burning type; the kind you saw only in Western movies in the United States. A long tongue of flame and a shower of sparks shot up into the air as Chris lifted one of the front lids and set the teakettle over the opening.

"When we first bought the place," Chris said, "we planned to install one of those newfangled electric stoves in a year or two. But we got attached to this old girl. We've never regretted it either. I don't know how many times the electric power has conked out for days at a time. Anyway, this cooks better than any gas or electric stove I've ever seen."

After they had eaten, they stacked the dishes in the sink and went out to the garage. Chris Hanson and Professor Stern were armed with .30-.30 Winchester rifles. Stern said their neighbor down the road had promised to provide weapons for the boys. They piled into the jeep, which had been warming up for a half hour, and drove about two miles into the foothills to the ranch of Vladimir

Thorsen, the son of a Russian-Swedish sourdough who had struck it rich in the gold rush. Thorsen was a short, rugged-looking man of fifty, with jet-black hair and a Vandyke beard. His English was precise, with just a trace of an accent. He welcomed the boys heartily and insisted that the men join him in a last cup of strong black coffee mixed with brandy.

"I don't think we will have to look far for our bear," he announced grimly. "Two nights ago, a big brute came right into the barnyard and carried off one of my lambs."

Chris Hanson whistled shrilly between his teeth. "He had his nerve, didn't he?"

"A cunning old monster," Thorsen said. "From the size of his footprints, I would estimate he weighs about 1,400 pounds. He has toes missing on his two forefeet."

"He's evidently been in some battles," Stern said. "And won them."

When the men had finished their coffee, Thorsen escorted them into his den. The walls were covered with pistols and rifles and the mounted heads of every kind of big game imaginable. The rancher took down two big, unwieldy, ancient-looking rifles and handed them to the boys. "Here are your weapons."

Sandy and Jerry couldn't help but show their disappointment. "They're very nice guns, sir." Sandy made an effort to sound appreciative. "But —what are they?"

"They look as if they were left over from the Revolutionary War," Professor Stern said tartly. "What are you trying to pull on these kids, Thorsen?"

Thorsen stroked his pointed beard and cast a reproving eye on the instructor. "You are an American teacher and you don't recognize this magnificent rifle! It is a Sharpe's buffalo gun, the same kind that your Buffalo Bill killed 1,800 buffalo with. I'm ashamed of you, Kenneth."

"It's only single-shot, too," Jerry observed critically.

"With a gun like that you only need one shot," Thorsen said. "You could drop an elephant with one shot." He opened a drawer of his desk and took out a handful of enormous cartridges. "See?"

Chris Hanson picked one up and hefted it in his palm. "It's a small artillery shell." He grinned at the boys. "You want to trade? I'd feel plenty safe facing Mr. Bear with this cannon."

"No," Jerry answered quickly. "If it was good enough for Buffalo Bill, it's good enough for me." He picked up one of the long rifles and balanced it on his shoulder. "Hup-two-three-four . . ." He staggered around the room. "Hey, doesn't a weapons carrier come with this thing?"

The rancher smiled, showing two rows of strong, white teeth. "You are a very funny fellow," he said. "Maybe the bear will die laughing. . . . Come, the horses are already saddled and waiting."

Jerry's face clouded over. "Horses?" he said.

"Yes, we may have to go ten or fifteen miles into the hills." He led them out of the den, through the kitchen and out the back door.

The boys fell behind as they approached the stables. "Have you ever ridden a horse before?" Jerry whispered to Sandy.

"Sure, I'm a fair rider." Realization suddenly dawned in his eyes. "You've ridden before— haven't you?"

"Only on the merry-go-round," Jerry said miserably. "But don't say anything. I don't want to spoil the party."

"Well . . ." Sandy was uncertain. "I suppose we'll be walking the horses mostly, so you can't get into too much trouble."

"Sure, we can hang back and you can instruct me in the fine points of horsemanship."

An Indian groom brought the horses out of the

stable. They were much sturdier animals than the ones Sandy had rented at any riding academy—more like cowboy ponies. They wore Western saddles, too.

"They're all mares," Thorsen explained. "Not too high-spirited and very manageable. Good mounts for tracking."

Jerry's eyes were round as he and his horse confronted each other. "This is the closest I've ever been to one," he confided to Sandy. "I never realized they were so big."

"You won't have any trouble," Sandy assured him. "She's a gentle girl." He stroked the smooth flanks and the muscles rippled beneath the glossy black coat. "Come on, I'll give you a lift."

Jerry mounted without difficulty and settled himself comfortably in the big saddle with his feet planted in the stirrups. "Nothing to it," he said.

Sandy grinned. "Nothing to a jet plane either, while it's sitting in the hangar. Here." He handed Jerry's rifle up to him.

"What do I do with it?" Jerry demanded.

Sandy indicated a large leather sheath that was fastened to the right side of the saddle. "Stick it in the saddle boot."

They rode out single file, with Thorsen's horse

breaking trail through knee-deep snow across a broad meadow behind the ranch house. A long split-rail fence ran along the back of the property. Thorsen pointed out a break in the fence, where the heavy logs lay scattered around like jackstraws and a six-inch post was snapped off at the base.

"That's where he came through."

From the break in the fence a wide path, which looked as if it had been plowed by a small bulldozer, led up a slope into a grove of spruce trees.

"It won't be much of a problem tracking him, will it?" Chris Hanson said.

Thorsen shrugged. "It depends. We're protected from the wind in the valley. Farther up in the mountains, the trail may be covered over by now. It's been two days."

Professor Stern swung down off his horse and knelt to examine the bear's footprints, which had been almost obliterated by blowing snow. He brushed away some of the fine, white powder with his mitten. Abruptly, he looked up at the rancher. "Did any one of your hands take a shot at this fellow?"

Thorsen frowned. "Certainly not. Why?"

Stern pointed to faint, rust-colored streaks in the snow between the imprints of the bear's foot pads. "Looks like blood to me. Probably a wound, high on the leg, and the blood trickled down between the toes."

"Maybe he hurt himself when he broke through the fence," Sandy suggested.

"That's possible," Stern conceded. He walked back and inspected the broken logs carefully. Finally, he shook his head. "No sign of blood here. I'm afraid our bear has been the victim of a careless hunter."

Thorsen scowled fiercely and muttered something in a guttural foreign tongue. Then he exploded in English. "I would like to get my hands on that filthy pig!"

"I don't get it," Jerry said to Sandy. "What's he so excited about? That's the whole idea, isn't it, to shoot the bear?"

"Sure, but once you wound an animal, it's your obligation to finish him off. That's the first commandment of hunting. First of all, it's cruel to let an animal suffer. And when you're dealing with big game, it's downright dangerous. A pain-crazed bear, for instance, can be a menace to anything that comes anywhere near him."

"That's right," Chris Hanson agreed. "We're going to have to stay on our toes from here on."

Professor Stern swung back into the saddle and they followed the bear's trail into the woods.

There were great, towering ancient pines, clustered together so that their heavy foliage meshed to form a solid roof above the forest floor. Only a fine dusting of snow had filtered through their heavy branches onto the thick carpet of pine needles that cushioned the earth. The horses' hoofbeats were barely audible as they picked their way between the trees, which were bare for at least twenty feet up.

"It's like being in a cathedral," Sandy said reverently. The voices of the men ahead sounded embarrassingly loud in the silence beneath the pines.

A pine cone skittered out from under the hoof of Jerry's horse and rattled across the dry needles. Jerry started and almost slipped out of the saddle.

"Watch it, boy," Sandy cautioned him. "How is it going, anyway?"

"I'll be okay, once old Dobbin and I get ourselves co-ordinated. Every time he goes up, I'm coming down and vice versa."

Sandy grinned. "You're too tense. Relax and try to imagine you're part of the horse."

"I know what part I feel like," Jerry said wryly.

On the other side of the grove they picked up the bear's trail again. It headed up a steep, rocky hillside, dotted with patches of scrubby trees and huge boulders. The horses had slippery footing and they went very slowly now.

Thorsen took his rifle out of the saddle boot, levered a shell into the chamber and rested it across the saddle in front of him. The other men followed suit.

Professor Stern turned and smiled reassuringly at the boys. "Don't be alarmed. It just doesn't pay to take any chances. I've heard of these wily old bears doubling back on their trail and setting up an ambush for unwary hunters."

Jerry swallowed hard and cast a nervous glance back over his shoulder. "Maybe it wasn't such a good idea to bring up the rear." His horse skidded unexpectedly on a mound of loose stones and Jerry clutched it frantically around the neck with both arms, burying his face in the thick mane. When the horse had steadied itself again, he straightened up and settled himself gingerly in the saddle.

He touched one hand to the seat of his pants and moaned. "How can one part of you feel so hot when the rest of you is so cold?"

Sandy was sympathetic. "Yeah, I feel for you, pal. That old saddle gets pretty hard after a while. And this is a rough way to get initiated to horseback riding to begin with."

They rode on for another half hour until they came to a shallow ravine with a dense growth of white birch trees and underbrush. Thorsen studied the steep rocky slopes of the ravine carefully. Except for a light dusting of snow they were wind-blown clean, as was the rocky shelf on the other side.

"I can't see any sign of a trail. For all we know, he may be hiding down there in those trees," he said.

Professor Stern nodded in agreement. "It's possible. I'd hate to run into a Kodiak in those close quarters. What do we do now?"

"We play it completely safe," Thorsen replied. "Some of us can ride around the ravine—it's no more than a quarter of a mile to the north—and see if we can pick up his trail on the other side. If we do, we can assume he's not waiting to pounce on us in the ravine. Those who remain here can safely ride across directly."

"Why don't we all ride around together?" Chris wanted to know. "What's the point of leaving anyone here?"

Thorsen stroked his silky beard. "Because if Mr. Bear *is* hiding in the ravine, we have him trapped. One group can flush him out into the guns of the other group."

"That seems sound," Stern acknowledged. "Which of us will stay here?"

"Jerry and I will," Sandy volunteered. "Both of us are pretty tired, and it'll give us a chance to rest."

"All right," Stern said. "Better make sure your guns are ready for action in case that bear surprises you."

As the three men rode off along the edge of the ravine, the boys dismounted and tethered their horses to a bare, crooked sapling. Sandy sat down on a boulder with his buffalo gun across his knees, but Jerry remained standing.

"I may never sit down again," he told Sandy.

Soon the three men passed out of sight where the ravine curved back behind a ridge, and the boys turned their attention to the birch trees below them.

"Think our bear is down there?" Sandy asked.

"Naw, I bet he's miles away from here by now."

The words were scarcely out of Jerry's mouth when the sound of a rock clattering down the far side of the ravine jerked their eyes upward. Standing beside a big boulder on the rocky shelf facing them was the biggest bear they had ever seen in their lives. His long, shaggy fur was tipped with silver, and on his underside it almost brushed the ground. The monster seemed oblivious of their presence.

"I don't think he sees us," Sandy whispered to Jerry. "They have very poor eyesight. And we're upwind of him so he can't smell us."

But the horses caught the scent of the bear and began to whinny and stamp their hoofs in terror. The big Kodiak's ears went up and he lifted his head, probing the air with his sensitive snout. Slowly he reared up on his hind legs.

Jerry couldn't restrain a gasp of astonishment and wonder. "Wow! Will you look at the size of him! He must be ten feet tall if he's an inch."

When the bear stood erect, Sandy could see a red, matted spot on his left shoulder. "Someone shot him all right," he said. He pressed his lips firmly together and lifted the big rifle to his shoulder. "Well, here goes." Then he added, "You take a bead on him too, Jerry, in case I miss."

"I'm so jittery, I don't think I *could* hit the side of a barn," Jerry answered breathlessly. Nevertheless, he brought up his rifle.

"It's an easy shot," Sandy told him. "Only about forty yards. I'll try for a head shot. You aim just below the left shoulder. And take off your mittens, idiot."

Sandy squinted down the long barrel, fixing the sight on a spot directly between the bear's eyes. Very gently he squeezed the trigger. There was a tremendous explosion and a numbing blow against his shoulder that sent him somersaulting backward off the boulder. He lay there stunned for an instant. Then Jerry grabbed the front of his parka and pulled him to his feet.

"What a recoil," Sandy mumbled.

"Forget the recoil!" Jerry was hopping up and down in excitement. "You got him! Look! One-shot Steele, that's you. Bet you could have made a chump out of Buffalo Bill."

Sandy focused his bleary eyes across the ravine. The Kodiak was just a big mound of motionless fur sprawled out on the ground.

"Come on!" Jerry pulled at Sandy's arm. "Let's hurry over there so we can make like big-game hunters when those other guys show up." Using his rifle as a staff, he started down the slope into the ravine.

Sandy caught up to him at the bottom and grabbed the rifle away from him. "Don't ever do anything like that again!" he snapped. "You dope! You might have blown your head off—or at least your hand. This is a loaded gun. You've got to have respect for it. Never point it at yourself or anyone else."

Jerry flushed and dropped his eyes. "Yeah, you're right. It was a dopey thing to do. I'm so crazy excited I forgot."

"Okay." Sandy handed the rifle back to him and they crashed through the brush and brambles that grew among the trunks of the birches. Scrambling up the far slope, Sandy was aware of a heavy weight banging against his right hip. He slipped his hand into his pocket on that side and touched the cold metal grip of the Colt automatic. He had forgotten about it when he packed the heavy parka away after the sled race.

He had just withdrawn his hand from his pocket when Jerry, who was in the lead, reached the top of the ravine. As his eyes cleared the rim, he stopped short and let out a wild yell. Then the bear lumbered into full view, looming over Jerry like a cat over a very small mouse. The monster's red-rimmed eyes blazed with hatred and Sandy could see pink foam gleaming on the long, bared fangs. It came to him as an incredible shock that here they were face to face with the most dangerous living thing in all the world—a wounded, pain-crazed Kodiak bear.

"Jerry! The gun! Shoot!" Sandy spat the words out jerkily.

Obeying mechanically, Jerry swung the long barrel up and fired in the same motion. The slug plowed harmlessly between the bear's legs, kicking up dirt and gravel. But it turned out to be a lifesaving shot. Caught off balance, Jerry was kicked off his feet by the booming recoil and went tumbling head over heels down the steep grade. At the same time Sandy drew out the big .45 pistol and cocked it. Then, as the bear dropped to all fours, with the obvious intention of attacking, Sandy fired at its hairy throat. The Army Colt .45-caliber packs a tremendous wallop. At such close range, it knocked the giant Kodiak back on its haunches.

Sandy pumped the last bullet into the bear's midsection, then turned and ran down the slope. Jerry was just getting to his feet when he reached the bottom of the ravine. "Find a tall tree and climb it," Sandy yelled. "Come on!"

Together they stumbled into the woods. Sandy remembered that on their way over they had passed one gnarled birch with a trunk as big around as a man's waist. In the manner of so many trees of this species, it had branched out into three thick, sturdy limbs at a height of about four feet. Without breaking his stride, Sandy leaped up, planted one foot in the crotch and clawed and shinnied his way up through the branches. He kept climbing until the limb began to bend beneath his weight. Then, with his heart fluttering like a frightened bird, he looked down, half expecting to see his friend in the embrace of the great bear. There was no trace of either Jerry or the Kodiak.

"Here I am," Jerry's voice rang out, so startlingly close that Sandy almost lost his hold on the branch. The sight of Jerry swaying back and forth on an adjacent limb at least five feet above him, arms and legs wrapped tightly around it like a monkey, made him weak with relief. In spite of their precarious position, he had to smile.

Jerry was appalled. "He's hysterical. Stark, raving mad," he cried. "Sandy! Snap out of it."

"I'm fine," Sandy said. "It's just that I didn't expect to see you up there."

"Where did you think I'd be? Back there, Indian-wrestling with old Smokey so you could escape?"

"I don't know how you got up there so fast. I didn't even see you pass me."

"Brother," Jerry said huffily, "if you had been as close to that critter as I was you'd be back in Valley View by now."

As yet there was still no sign of the bear on the ground below them. Sandy searched the rocky shelf where they had encountered him, but it was empty. The clatter of horses' hoofs drew his attention back to the side of the ravine they had come from. Professor Stern and the other two men came galloping into view and reined in their horses.

"Here, in the tree!" Sandy hailed them. "We're up in the tree."

Stern's face reflected his relief—and not a little amazement. "What on earth are you doing in a tree? And what were those shots we heard?"

"We shot the bear. Then he came to life again and chased us up here." Sensing the professor's understandable confusion, he grinned. "I guess that sounds pretty wild, doesn't it?"

"Indeed it does," Stern admitted. "But never mind that. Where is the bear now?"

"I don't know."

Thorsen and Chris Hanson were already starting down into the ravine, rifles ported for action. Stern dismounted and followed them. Cautiously the men made their way through the trees. Before they reached the far side of the ravine the boys lost sight of them.

After several minutes of complete silence, Sandy began to get anxious.

"Maybe that old bear was hiding behind a tree," Jerry suggested, "and clobbered each one of them as they went by him, like the Indians used to do."

Finally they heard Stern's voice calling to them. "You guys can come down now."

Sandy was puzzled. "That's funny. I guess the bear got away after all." He slid hurriedly to the ground.

When they emerged from the birch grove, both boys stopped dead. Sandy shut his eyes tight, opened them, shut them, and opened them again. He couldn't believe what he saw. The three men were standing at the bottom of the slope, all flashing broad grins. At their feet was the mountainous carcass of the bear.

"You—you sure he's dead?" Sandy stammered.

"Yeah," Jerry said. "He's a tricky one."

Thorsen jabbed his toe into the shaggy body. "Quite dead, I assure you, my young friends."

"We had just reached the end of the ravine when we heard the shots," Professor Stern said. "Now tell us what happened."

Both talking at once, the boys recited the story of their escapade with the big Kodiak.

"You remember that old movie *King Kong*, where the girl first sees this giant gorilla?" Jerry asked. "Well, that's how I felt when this thing came at me. Oh broth-er!" He shuddered.

Sandy took out the black Colt pistol. "And this is what saved our lives."

Thorsen took it from him and examined it admiringly. "A true gem. Do you know how this gun was developed? During the Philippine Insurrection, American troops were being demoralized by fierce Moro tribesmen, savage warriors who carried wicked bolo knives. The Moros would pop up out of the jungle without warning and attack the soldiers at such close quarters that it was impossible for them to use their rifles. And the Moros were so physically powerful that the average pistol couldn't stop them. Even with a half dozen bullets in them, they could decapitate an enemy with their bolos before they died. The Army Colt .45 was designed especially to stop them. And it did the job well—with one slug."

"It certainly stopped this monster," said Chris Hanson.

"But it was a very lucky shot," Professor Stern tempered his praise. "The first shot you fired with the rifle creased his skull and stunned him. He was probably still whoozy when you ran into him, or you might not have had a chance to get in a second shot. Your last shot severed the jugular vein. It was a very lucky shot," he emphasized.

"You don't have to convince me, Professor," Sandy said soberly. "As of now I am a retired bear hunter."

CHAPTER THIRTEEN

The Ghost Mine

TWO DAYS LATER the Sterns and the Hansons came down to the airstrip to see the boys off. Professor Stern promised to send the bearskin to Valley View as soon as it was cured. "It will make a nice trophy to spread out in front of your fireplace," he told Sandy.

"I think I'll donate it to our local boys' club," Sandy said.

"And every time a new fellow joins up, he'll have an excuse to tell what a big hero he is," Jerry joked.

Sandy laughed. "I bet I looked like a big hero up in that tree all right."

Russ Parker appeared in the doorway of the

plane. "All revved up and ready to go. You fellows set?"

The boys said their last goodbyes and climbed into the cabin.

Mrs. Stern waved and yelled, "Thanks again for refilling my freezer."

"We'll eat it up the next time we come," Jerry said.

Parker slammed the door and bolted it, then went forward to the cockpit. "Fasten your safety belts," he ordered. The little plane took off smoothly and climbed over the bay. Through the window next to him, Sandy caught a last glimpse of the twin domes of the Russian church and the ancient sea wall with its great iron rings where the fur traders used to tie up their ships. The sun sparkled on the blue water and glinted briefly off the metal oil tanks of the U.S. naval base far across the bay. Parker leveled off at 10,000 feet and set a northeast course.

Sandy unbuckled his seat belt and went up front to the cockpit. "How long will it take to fly to Cordova?" he inquired.

"With this tail wind no more than two hours," Parker said. "We should be landing a little after ten. Your dad and the professor want to fly back to Juneau this afternoon."

Sandy nodded. "From there we're taking a commercial airline back to Seattle."

Parker put the ship on automatic pilot and turned sideways in the seat. "Not driving back down the highway?"

"No. Professor Crowell decided the trip was too rugged in the winter. He's leaving his dogs up here until spring. Anyway, Jerry and I have to get back to school, so we were planning to fly back in any case."

Listening to the conversation with one ear, Jerry looked up from the book he was reading. "Hey, Sandy, back in Valley View the guys are just steeling themselves for a session with Miss Remson in English Four. Isn't that great? And here we are three thousand miles away and two miles in the air. Think we're safe from her?"

"Sure," Sandy said. "And Miss Remson would probably be just as glad if you stayed that far away from her."

Parker pointed out a range of mountains just visible on the northwest horizon. "Too bad you don't have time to visit the Valley of Ten Thousand Smokes."

"That's an interesting name. What is it?"

"Before Mount Katmai erupted in 1912 it was a fertile farm region. Then the whole top of the mountain blew off—two cubic miles of rock vaporized into thin air. One hundred miles away in Kodiak they had to shovel the dust and ashes off the roof tops."

Sandy whistled. "That's as bad as having an H-bomb drop in your back yard."

"Maybe worse," Parker said grimly. "Then the entire floor of the valley erupted into little fumaroles, or volcanic potholes, that spewed out molten sand. Thousands of them. That's where they got the name Ten Thousand Smokes. Today there are only seven of them that are still active, but the valley is a desert wasteland."

Sandy squinted through the windshield, imagining he could see a thin ribbon of smoke rising from one of the peaks. "What happened to old Mount Katmai? Is it still active?"

"Well, the experts think it's still boiling way down inside. There's a big lake in the crater now, but it never freezes. I've heard it's warm enough to swim in."

Jerry, who had come forward to listen to the story, was wonderstruck. "Why, I bet you could land a plane on the lake and find out," he said.

"It's a thought," Parker agreed, not too enthusiastically. "Maybe some day I'll try it."

For the remainder of the trip, he captivated the

boys with other tales about the big land, and almost before they knew it they were approaching Cordova. The traffic was light and the tower gave them immediate clearance to land.

A quarter of an hour after the plane touched down, they were on their way to town in the auto of a radio technician who was going off duty. Russ Parker remained at the field to give the Norseman a thorough inspection before the afternoon flight to Juneau. "We'll take off about one, I guess," he told them as they were leaving.

The considerate radio man dropped them off in front of the old-fashioned hotel where Dr. Steele had said they would be staying. The clerk at the desk informed them that the geologists were still registered, but that he had not seen them since the previous morning.

"Are you certain they didn't come back when you were off duty?" Sandy asked him.

"Positive," the clerk declared. "The chambermaid said their beds haven't been slept in."

Sandy looked at Jerry helplessly. "Well, I guess we'll just have to wait for them."

The clerk gave them a passkey to one of the two adjoining rooms occupied by Dr. Steele and his party. When they entered the room, the boys were surprised to see that the geologists hadn't even started to pack. Clothing, books and toilet articles were scattered everywhere.

Jerry looked at his wrist watch. "We're never going to take off for Juneau at one o'clock at this rate. It's after eleven now. Are you sure you didn't get the days mixed up, Sandy? Maybe your father wasn't expecting us until tomorrow."

A little seed of fear began to grow inside of Sandy. "No, he said the third. Professor Crowell told Russ he wanted to fly to Juneau today, too. I can't understand it, Jerry. If Dad didn't expect to be here when we got back from Kodiak, he would have left word for us. Anyway, they couldn't have been planning to make any overnight trips. They didn't take razors, toothbrushes or anything; my dad shaves every morning even when he's on a fishing trip miles from civilization. I don't like it, Jerry."

Jerry's face turned pale under its perpetual tan. "Sandy, you don't think those enemy agents . . . ?" He left the sentence unfinished.

Before Sandy could reply, the telephone on the stand between the twin beds jangled harshly. The boys looked at each other hopefully.

"Maybe that's Dad calling." Sandy threw himself across one of the beds and picked up the receiver eagerly. But it was Russ Parker phoning from the airfield.

"I don't think it's anything to worry about," Parker said, "but I just found out that your dad and his friends chartered a plane yesterday morning to fly out to McCarthy. That's an old ghost town near the abandoned Kennecott copper mine. When they didn't show back last night, the authorities figured they had been forced down somewhere with engine trouble. Search planes have been combing the area all morning, but there's no sign of the plane, crashed or otherwise."

"What do you think we should do, Russ?" Sandy asked in a tight voice.

"I dunno. I sort of thought we might fly out that way ourselves and have a look."

"That's a good idea, Russ. Jerry and I will be out as soon as we can hitch a ride. Thanks for calling." He slammed down the receiver and related the latest development to Jerry. Minutes later they were on their way.

As they swooped low across the small ghost town of McCarthy, Parker banked the plane sharply and indicated the unblemished expanses of white around the town. "No one has set down here since before the last snow," he said.

"Is there anywhere else they might have landed?" Sandy asked.

"Maybe up at the mine proper. We'll fly up that way and have a look."

"Imagine having a ghost town up here," Jerry marveled. "I thought they were exclusive to the old American West. It's kind of spooky, everyone packing up and leaving a place. Almost as if it was haunted."

"Ghost towns are haunted in a sense," Sandy said. "By poverty and hunger. They're towns that build up around mines and have no other livelihood. If the mines close down they're doomed."

"Any community that puts all its eggs in one basket runs the risk of becoming a ghost town," Parker put in.

"Why did the Kennecott mine shut down?" Sandy asked curiously.

"The ore just ran out," Parker said. "Here we are now."

Below them Sandy saw a sprawling shedlike structure that seemed to be hanging on the side of a hill. "That's the main building," Parker said. "See those long wires that look like trolley cables? They used to send the ore down from the shafts by cable car. Then it was loaded on trains and shipped to Cordova to be put on ships."

On a level plateau below the Kennecott mine, they spotted the long twin ski marks of a plane. There were two sets, one set almost parallel to the other.

"No doubt about it," Parker said. "A plane landed here recently. And it took off again." He brought the Norseman's nose up and began climbing.

"But if they took off again, where *did* they go?" Sandy was sick with fear. The idea of his father lying badly injured—or worse—in the wreckage of a crashed plane terrified him. "If—if they had cracked up, the search planes would have found them by now, wouldn't they?"

Parker chewed thoughtfully on his underlip. "I would think so. Unless they wandered outlandishly far off course. But there isn't any reason why they should have. The last two days and nights have been perfect for flying." Ominously, he added, "But we can't discount that possibility altogether. There's so much territory to cover even with an air search that a small plane might be missed. In Canada they insist that private planes follow well-traveled routes like the Alaska Highway instead of flying the beam, for that very reason. If you have to make a forced landing, there's a better chance you'll be found promptly."

"Listen," Sandy implored the pilot, "let's land here and look around. Maybe we'll find a clue or something to show where they went."

Parker shrugged. "Sure, if it'll make you feel any better. But if they were here, they definitely took off again."

Parker landed the Norseman smoothly, cutting across the ski tracks of the other plane. He taxied to the far end of the clearing, turning her about in position for a take-off, then cut the engines. The plane settled heavily in the snow.

"Looks pretty deep out there," Parker estimated. "We better dig out snowshoes from the baggage compartment."

They had landed about a quarter of a mile away from the main building of the mine, and because of the boys' inexperience on snowshoes it was a slow walk.

"I feel just like a duck," Jerry grumbled as he brought up the rear, flopping along in the clumsy, webbed footgear. "Overgrown tennis rackets, that's all they are."

"You're not supposed to try and walk the way you do in shoes," Sandy instructed him. "You just shuffle along."

At last they stood beneath the big ramshackle structure. It *was* spooky, Sandy had to admit to himself, just as Jerry said. Once this building had been the nerve center of a booming industry, buzzing with activity and life. Now it stood on the hillside, gaunt, decaying and silent. Before many more years it would become a rickety skeleton.

He shuddered as Parker led them up on the moldy loading platform and into the tomblike dampness of the shed. "We can go on up to the main building through here. There are stairs right inside." They passed through a doorway into a room illuminated only by the slivers of daylight that penetrated the cracked boards.

Suddenly, Russ Parker did an about-face and began talking. "Well, here we are." Only he seemed to be talking to someone in back of them.

Sandy whirled quickly and saw that the doorway was blocked by a huge man wearing a stocking cap and a plaid mackinaw. His face was hidden in shadow. But the big Lüger pistol in his right hand was very plain to see.

CHAPTER FOURTEEN

The Plot Revealed

IN HIS OTHER HAND the stranger carried a square electric lantern. He turned the powerful beam on Sandy and Jerry. "Did you have any trouble with them, Parker?"

"Not a bit," Parker said. "The Steele boy suggested himself that we land here. And of course there was no trouble at all persuading him to fly out here with me."

The boys looked from Parker to the other man in bewilderment. "Russ," Sandy pleaded, "tell us what's going on. Who is this guy?" He turned on the stranger belligerently. "Do you know where my father is?"

"My name is Kruger," the man snapped. "And,

167

yes, I do know where your father is. Now, turn around and march up those stairs." He waved the pistol at them threateningly.

As the boys started up the stairs, the men fell behind and lowered their voices. "How do you like that!" Jerry declared. "Russ Parker is in with these characters."

"I can hardly believe it," Sandy said miserably. "Anyhow, at least I know Dad is okay—so far," he amended.

"No conversation, please," Kruger ordered sharply.

"Parker, you sneak," Sandy said bitterly, "you won't get away with this. The authorities know my dad and his friends are missing. And when we don't show back at the airfield there'll be even more search planes combing this area."

The pilot began to laugh. "No one knows your father and the others are missing. No one at all. By now the hotel has received a telegram from Skagway saying that Professor Crowell and his party returned there on urgent business and that someone will pick up their luggage and pay their hotel bill."

Sandy was confused. "But—but what about the people at the airport? You said there were search planes out looking for the missing plane."

"There is no missing plane. Yesterday morning four men rented a plane. Last evening the plane returned—with four men. There was another crew on duty at the airport. They couldn't suspect that the passengers were four *different* men."

Kruger seemed to enjoy the boys' discomfort. "By the time the American authorities discover that any of you are missing you will be well out of reach in Siberia."

"Across that narrow stretch of water we were talking about," Parker taunted them. "The Bering Strait."

The man with the gun took them through a series of tunnels that slanted up steeply through the mountainside. The ascent was severe, and every ten minutes or so they would stop to rest. When they emerged into the open again, Sandy saw that they were at the site of the main diggings. The terrain was pockmarked with shafts and tunnels. Rusty train tracks disappeared into the gloomy mine tunnels, and abandoned dump cars tilted up through the snow drifts about the entrances. Far below, the main building of the Kennecott mine squatted at the foot of the mountain; from this perspective it reminded Sandy of a miniature cardboard house sitting on a floor of cotton beneath a Christmas tree. They followed a path around a bend to the mouth of a huge tunnel. To one side of it a flaking, rusted cable car rocked gently from a metal cable that was equally rusted. It scraped and screeched monotonously at the slightest gust of wind.

"In here," Kruger ordered. "This was one of the main shafts of the mine."

They walked along the rail ties back about one hundred yards, where a rectangle of yellow light splashed into the corridor from a doorway in one wall of the tunnel. Kruger motioned them through the doorway into a big chamber that evidently had served as a locker room for the miners. Rotting wooden benches and tin lockers cluttered up the room, many of them overturned, all of them sagging. A large gasoline lantern burned on a long wooden table in the middle of the room. On either side of the table sat a strange man with a rifle across his knees. Across the table, seated all in a row on a bench, their hands and feet tied, were Dr. Steele, Professor Crowell, Lou Mayer and Tagish Charley.

"Dad!" Sandy burst out. "Am I glad to see you! Are you okay?"

Dr. Steele managed a strained smile. "I'm all right, Son. We all are. But I can't say I'm glad to see you boys." He turned to one of the men with the rifles. "Did you have to drag them into it, Strak? They're only boys. They don't even know what this is all about."

The man he addressed, a short, intense fellow who moved with the quick, nervous motions of a squirrel, stood up and walked toward the new arrivals. He stopped in front of Sandy and stroked his prominent clean-shaven chin.

"So this is your son, Dr. Steele? A fine-looking lad." He spoke careful, formal English. "I, too, regret that he and the other youth had to become involved. But we couldn't take any chances. They would have notified the police that you were missing and . . ."

"Don't be a fool!" Professor Crowell snapped. "The police will discover our absence soon enough."

Strak smiled patiently. "I disagree. Secrecy has been the keynote of your project. Only a few people in both your governments—high officials —know your real purpose in coming to Alaska. By the time they discover you are missing, we will all be safely out of the country."

"Of course, Dr. Steele, you could spare your son and his friend a lot of unnecessary hardship by co-operating with us," Kruger said. "Just the answer to one simple question . . ."

"You're wasting your time," Dr. Steele said flatly.

"Have it your own way." Strak sighed wearily. "You will tell us, you know. That is certain. To-day, tomorrow, next week or six months from now. We can wait."

Kruger pushed the boys toward the bench where the other hostages were seated. "Parker, help me tie these two up."

When the boys were securely bound, Strak motioned Parker to follow him. "Come, Parker. Let us go outside. We have a few things to discuss in private."

"You want Malik and me to stay here and guard the prisoners?" Kruger asked.

Strak hesitated a moment, then shook his head. "No, come along. You should all hear this." He glanced at the prisoners. "I don't think they'll get loose." He smiled. "And even if they did, where would they go? We'll be up at the entrance—the only entrance."

The four men left the room and their footsteps echoed off down the tunnel. In the dim light of the lantern Dr. Steele's face was drawn and pale.

"I'll never forgive myself, getting you boys mixed up in this," he said. "Once I knew they were on to us, that we hadn't deceived them into thinking this was an innocent geological expedition, I should have sent you back to California on the first plane."

"Don't blame yourself, Dad," Sandy said quietly. "I wouldn't have left you, knowing that you were in some kind of serious trouble."

"That goes for me too, sir," Jerry backed him up.

"What I don't understand," Sandy said, "is how they caught you."

"We walked right into their hands," Professor Crowell explained. "Parker knew we were coming up to the Kennecott mine and tipped them off. They flew up ahead of us, hid their plane in the trees and covered up the ski tracks. When we arrived they were waiting for us."

"A whole gang of them," Lou Mayer put in. "Seven of them, armed to the teeth. Four of them took our plane back to Cordova so the people at the airport wouldn't report us missing."

"I know," Sandy said grimly. "They took care of the hotel too. By the time the authorities get suspicious it will be too late. The one called Kruger says we'll be in Russia by then."

Dr. Steele and Professor Crowell looked at each other hopelessly. "Unless we tell them what they want to know," Dr. Steele said.

Sandy's eyes were puzzled. "Just what are they after? I guess you can tell us now."

Dr. Steele smiled wanly. "I guess we can." He paused before he went on. "Although he's better known as a geologist, Professor Crowell is one of Canada's leading physicists. During World War Two he was assigned to rocket research work for the Canadian Army and continued to specialize in this field after the war.

"About six months ago an old Yukon prospector submitted an ore sample to a government assay office at Whitehorse. He said he had been prospecting on the Alaskan border and struck what he believed was a vein of gold. An analysis of the sample revealed traces of copper, but no gold. But much more important, it revealed strains of a rare element that the Canadian government was testing as a catalytic agent in top-secret experiments with a new solid rocket fuel.

"For years now rocket experts have acknowledged that solid fuels are more practical than liquid propellants—even more so for the big manned rocket ships of the future. The trouble is, up until now the solid fuels haven't been too dependable. Professor Crowell believes this new element will solve the most serious drawbacks, but unhappily it's about as rare as uranium. During the past few months there have been teams out searching for it all over the Dominion, without much success.

"Then, unexpectedly, this old prospector shows up with an ore sample laced liberally with it. The assay office at Whitehorse dispatched it to Ottawa immediately and Professor Crowell was consulted. It was his opinion that they were on to something big. A special agent flew up to Whitehorse to interview the prospector, but tragically —any way you look at it—the poor old man had passed away from pneumonia only a few days before the agent arrived.

"Now the big problem was to find out where the dead man had picked up the ore. All kinds of soil and rock analyses were made on it without any specific results. It was the professor's guess that it came from somewhere in the vicinity of the Kennecott copper mine. There was copper in the sample, of course, and the old miner had mentioned vaguely at the assay office that he had discovered it somewhere 'on the border.' A layman couldn't be expected to know exactly where the border lies; actually, he may have wandered well into Alaska.

"In any case, the Canadian government conferred with Washington, and it was decided to send a joint team up to Alaska composed of Professor Crowell, Lou Mayer and myself." He glanced toward the doorway and added sourly, "We didn't count on it ending up a three-nation team."

"How did they find out?" Sandy wanted to know.

Dr. Steele shrugged. "They have the most efficient espionage system in the world. That we have to give them credit for."

Sandy pursed his lips solemnly. "But they still don't know what the element is?"

"Or how it's employed in the manufacture of the rocket fuel," Professor Crowell declared emphatically. "I'm the only one who can tell them that. And I'll die first."

"Watch it," Jerry cautioned. "I think I hear them coming back."

The sound of approaching footsteps reverberated hollowly through the mine. Strak appeared in the doorway alone. "Kruger and Malik have gone down the mountain to help Parker clear a runway," he told them. "We'll be taking off with a heavy load."

Sandy made a quick mental count. "That plane will never get off the ground with ten of us."

Strak smiled. "I agree. But there are only seven of us who will be making the trip."

"What do you mean?" Dr. Steele demanded.

"Just that you and your son and Professor Crowell are the only ones who have any real value to us. The rest will remain here."

Dr. Steele was shocked. "You can't intend to leave them tied up in this mine? They'll starve to death or die of exposure."

Strak shrugged. "That's a risk we will have to take. Perhaps in time they may be able to get loose. Perhaps they will make it back to civilization. Who can tell? The Indian seems to be a resourceful woodsman." He walked over and stood in front of Tagish Charley. "Tell me, Doctor, he *is* alive, isn't he?"

Tagish Charley's face betrayed no trace of emotion. He had not spoken a word since the boys' arrival. All the while he had sat stiffly on the bench, hands behind him, eyes staring fixedly at the rock wall in front of him—as detached as any cigar-store Indian could be, or so it seemed to Sandy.

In sudden irritation Strak bent close to Charley, flashing his electric torch into his face. "You insolent Indian dog! You can speak, can't you?"

Then, for the first time, Charley showed some sign of life. Slowly he lifted his eyes to Strak's face and said solemnly, "Charley too busy to talk

—until *now!*" As he shouted the last word, his two powerful arms whipped free from behind him and wrapped around his tormentor.

Strak tried desperately to bring up his rifle, but he was helpless in Charley's grizzly-bear hug. The air whistled out of his lungs like a wheezing bellows, and there was the distinct snap of a rib cracking. He moaned softly and fainted. Charley let him drop to the floor.

"Atta boy, Charley!" Jerry said exultantly.

They all winced as the Indian held up his hands in the light. His wrists were raw and bleeding from rubbing at the rope. "Big spike in bench where I sit. Slow work, but at end I saw rope through." He bent over Strak and removed a hunting knife from the man's belt. Quickly he cut through the ropes that bound his own ankles. Then he went along the bench freeing the others.

"Come on!" Dr. Steele said, grabbing up Strak's rifle from the ground. "No time to lose. The others will be coming back soon." He led the way out of the room and down the tunnel to the entrance.

At the foot of the mountain beyond the abandoned mine building, they could see the plane sitting like a toy in the snow. The three enemy agents were bustling around it, mere specks at this distance.

"They're still working on the runway," Sandy observed.

"What do we do when they come back?" Jerry asked.

Lou Mayer indicated the rifle the doctor was holding. "We have one gun. We can make a fight of it at least."

Dr. Steele was not enthusiastic. "All three of them are armed. I'm afraid it wouldn't be much of a fight." His voice was grim. "Some of us would be hurt—or killed."

"Why couldn't we rush down the hill when we see them start up?" Professor Crowell suggested. "They'd be inside, coming up through the shafts. By the time they got up here, we'd have quite a head start on them. If we get to that plane—"

Dr. Steele shook his head. "We'd never stand a chance without snowshoes, and they're all down at the mine shed. They'd have a field day picking us off with their rifles while we flounder through those hip-deep drifts on the mountain."

"Then we've got no choice," Lou Mayer said gloomily. "We've got to make a stand here."

"Wait a minute!" Sandy cried out, the bud of

a wild inspiration forming in his mind. "Is there any chance *that* thing still works?" The others followed his gaze upward to the old cable car creaking and rocking to the right of the entrance.

The professor sighed. "I'm afraid not. These cable cars were operated by power machinery down at the depot."

"I know," Sandy said. "But we'd be coasting downhill."

There was a gleam of interest in Dr. Steele's eyes. "That sounds logical. What do you say we have a look at it, Son? But keep down. We don't want Kruger and the others to spot us against the snow."

They slunk out of the shadow of the mine entrance, darting quickly behind the cover of the cable car. Dr. Steele climbed into the open cab and squinted up at the rigging. "Looks to me as if the only thing that's restraining it is that safety lock," he said.

Sandy disagreed. "What about the pulley cable? That must be anchored in the shed below. She won't roll unless that's free."

Dr. Steele studied the arrangement of rollers and cables more closely. "You're right," he admitted. He pointed to the steel hook-eye at the back of the car where the pulley cable was attached. "The wire is pretty frayed back here. Possibly we could hack through it. I saw an old ax back in the cave."

"It's sure worth a try," Sandy said. "How do you think that overhead cable will hold up when we start rolling downhill?"

"I'd say it's in pretty good condition. They put a good coating of grease on all the machinery before they shut the mine down. They must have hoped to use it again, or possibly to sell it."

Professor Crowell's voice rang out urgently from the tunnel entrance. "Hurry up! Kruger and the others are starting back."

Dr. Steele pulled Sandy down out of sight in the car. "We'll stay here until they enter the shed." He called over to Tagish Charley, "Charley, duck back into the mine and get a couple of those picks that are lying around."

Peering over the rim of the cable car, Sandy watched the three men make their way on snowshoes back to the mine. As soon as they had disappeared into the shed, Dr. Steele shouted for the others. "Come on, we've got to work fast. Charley, over here with those picks, quickly!"

Lou Mayer, Professor Crowell and Jerry scrambled aboard the car while Dr. Steele gave instructions to Tagish Charley. "You work on the hook-eye and pulley, Charley. I'll knock out the safety lock. The rest of you just pray."

One solid blow tripped the safety lock, and the car moved forward about a foot until the taut cable stopped it. The cable itself was more of a problem. Sandy had the uncomfortable sensation that his leaping heart was trying to squirm out of his throat and escape from his body.

The tension was unbearable as Charley pounded away at the pulley with strong rhythmic strokes of the ax. At first it seemed impervious to the dull blade. Then, with relief, Sandy saw one strand snap with a musical twang. Charley swung harder, encouraged by this success, and another strand broke. Each strand that let go put additional stress on the remaining strands, making Charley's task a little easier. The last two snapped together with a loud report.

The car shuddered and began to roll forward slowly. There was the nerve-shattering screech of metal against metal as the overhead rollers and the main cable protested violently at being used so rudely after twenty-one years of inactivity. Snow, rust and metal shavings cascaded down on the car's occupants as it picked up momentum.

The boys let go with a tremendous cheer and Professor Crowell and Dr. Steele shook hands solemnly. Sandy glanced behind them at the rapidly diminishing tunnel entrance, but as yet there was no sign of Kruger and the other two enemy agents.

Fortunately the pitting of the cable and the rust and stiffness of the rollers reduced their acceleration sufficiently so that they crashed into the bumpers at the foot of the incline with only a moderate jolt. The cable car split the rotting wood on the bumper's face, but the springs behind it cushioned the jolt.

Sandy extricated himself from the mass of scrambled limbs gingerly. "Everybody okay? No broken bones?"

There was a chorus of relieved okays.

Dr. Steele climbed out into the snow. "All right. Into the shed and on with those snowshoes." Apprehensively, he looked up the mountain, but the enemy agents still had not appeared.

As Sandy strapped on the great clumsy snowshoes, he made a suggestion. "Let's take the other four pairs with us. That will slow them up even more if they try to follow us."

"Good idea," Tagish Charley grunted. "But I got better one." He picked up the ax he had carried with him from the cable car and began to attack the surplus snowshoes furiously. When he had demolished them, he straightened up and, to everyone's amazement, grinned broadly. "They no go very far now."

They were halfway to the plane when a distant gunshot came to them faintly through the thin, dry air. Turning, Sandy could make out three ant-like specks on the mountainside near the tunnel where they had been held prisoner.

"They've discovered we're gone," he said.

"And they're shooting at us," Jerry commented nervously.

"We're not in much danger at this range," Professor Crowell assured them. "Without telescopic sights, it would take a mighty lucky shot to hit anyone."

Nevertheless, they were all greatly relieved when they were seated snugly in the cabin of the plane and Professor Crowell had the motors gunning smoothly. "Those fellows did a mighty fine job on this runway," the professor said charitably. He advanced the throttle and the ship glided ahead smoothly. They cleared the trees at the far end of the clearing with plenty of room to spare and climbed in a sweeping curve that took them over the mountain. Far below on the snowy slope they could see the frustrated agents hopping about and shaking their fists in the air.

CHAPTER FIFTEEN

Final Victory

"THEY'VE CAUGHT THE ENTIRE GANG!" Dr. Steele reported excitedly as he burst into the boys' hotel room at Cordova a little after eight the next morning.

Sandy sat up and massaged the sleep from his eyes. "No kidding, Dad. When?"

"Army Intelligence moved in on Strak, Parker and the other two at dawn. They gave up without a fight. Seems they put in a pretty rough night. Strak was in bad shape, thanks to Charley, but he'll live to stand trial for espionage."

"What about the rest of the gang?"

"The local police arrested them as they were trying to board a freighter at Valdez. It's a clean sweep."

"Wow!" Jerry was awake now, his eyes as big and shiny as tin plates. "That's what I call action." Grinning, he added, "We sure could have used a little bit of that kind of action yesterday. Where were all the cops and G-men then?"

"In an operation like this one," Dr. Steele explained, "they had to stay way out on the fringes until the last moment. That was a risk we knew we'd have to take from the start if we hoped to spring a trap on this gang of ruthless saboteurs. If we had an army of bodyguards dogging our footsteps, they never would have been lured in."

"Lured in?" Sandy was perplexed. "You mean we were sort of decoys for the spies?"

"In a way," Dr. Steele admitted. "I couldn't tell you that, even yesterday. But now it's officially okay to let you in on it."

"But what about the rocket fuel Professor Crowell was working on? I thought we came up to look for some rare element."

"That of course was our primary reason for coming to Alaska. And of course we'll continue to search for Element X. But when the enemy agents began to hound us so persistently, we saw an opportunity to make a double killing."

Jerry stretched. "Only we came awful close to being the ones who were killed."

"We had a narrow scrape," Dr. Steele agreed. "It was ingenious of them to take back the plane to Cordova after they ambushed us at the mine. Our people were holding back, of course, and it really threw them off the trail. As far as they knew, we had checked back into the city and then disappeared into thin air. With a bit more luck the gang might have smuggled us out of the country."

Jerry laughed. "Hey, Sandy, can you see us going to school in Siberia?"

"Frankly, no," Sandy told him. "You have enough trouble with English."

Dr. Steele broke in with "That reminds me. We have to think of getting you boys back to Valley View. You don't want to miss too much more school."

"Speak for yourself, Doctor," Jerry crowed. "How can you expect us to go back and associate with little school kids after battling Yukon blizzards, Kodiak bears and spies? It's positively undignified."

Dr. Steele smiled tolerantly. "Don't feel that way, Jerry. Remember, adventure and excitement may be just around the corner, whether you're in Alaska or California."

"Yeah, that's right," Jerry said thoughtfully.

Then he added, with a gleam in his eye, "Besides, it'll be great to come up with our story when Pepper March starts spouting about that cruise he was supposed to take. Boy, will *his* eyes pop! And you know what? We might even be able to stump Quiz Taylor. Wouldn't that be something? Okay, Valley View, here we come! How about it, Sandy?"

Sandy stretched blissfully. "I'm ready. In fact, I'm way ahead of you. How about next summer? Any ideas?"